THE OTHER ME

THE OTHER ME

A STORY OF TWO LIVES CHANGED FOREVER

Judy Tabs

 iUniverse®

THE OTHER ME
A STORY OF TWO LIVES CHANGED FOREVER

iUniverse books may be ordered through booksellers or by contacting:

iUniverse
1663 Liberty Drive
Bloomington, IN 47403
www.iuniverse.com
1-800-Authors (1-800-288-4677)

Because of the dynamic nature of the Internet, any web addresses or links contained in this book may have changed since publication and may no longer be valid. The views expressed in this work are solely those of the author and do not necessarily reflect the views of the publisher, and the publisher hereby disclaims any responsibility for them.

Any people depicted in stock imagery provided by Getty Images are models, and such images are being used for illustrative purposes only. Certain stock imagery © Getty Images.

ISBN: 978-1-5320-4923-1 (sc)
ISBN: 978-1-5320-4924-8 (e)

Library of Congress Control Number: 2018905699

Print information available on the last page.

iUniverse rev. date: 05/24/2018

AUTHOR'S NOTES

THE OTHER ME is a work of fiction, even though parts of it are a memoir taken from my grandson's experiences as a heart transplant recipient. When you read the book you will travel with me through the highs and lows of both the donor and recipient's families.

The New Jersey Sharing Network is a real organization that is committed to saving lives through the donation of organs and tissues.

A heartfelt thank you to my family and friends who helped and supported me through this literary journey.

PRAISES FOR THE OTHER ME

"*Thoughtful and compassionate viewpoints from both the donor and recipient families*
Beverly Silverman, LCSW

"*Enjoy it, Learn from it, Cry and Laugh with it…..READ IT!!!*"
Robin Goldman, Organ Recipient

"*I read it in one sitting.*"
Joanna Orland, student, S. I. Newhouse School of Communications, Syracuse University

"*Cell Memory is a fascinating area worthy of study*",
Ben Turetzky Executive Director of FOLKS, Friends of Lake Keowee Society.

"*This insightful book paints a vivid picture of both the tragedy of loss and the exhilaration of renewal.*",
Eileen Lurie,retired adjunct professor at Kean College.

"*THE OTHER ME is perfect for a book club selection. I will certainly recommend it to mine.*"
Wilma Odell, book club member, S.L.C.

DEDICATION

**This book is dedicated to my grandchildren
Max, Isabel, Alec and Sam**

**A special dedication to Sam whose bravery and
beautiful nature inspired me to write this book.**

Dedicated to all Donor families for
unselfishly giving the Gift of Life

CONTENTS

PREFACE

When we are born, life's three-ringed, soft-covered lined notebook is empty, and each day, month, and year, it slowly gets filled with our comings and goings, chronicling our story. Many factors contribute to the story: our family and friends, our health, our celebrations, our circumstances, and our communities. This is the story of two young New Jersey boys, Scott Paterson of Verona and David Goldman of Cedar Grove, who live only five miles from each other. Scott and David never meet, but their lives are completely changed on the same day—the day Hurricane Sandy hits New Jersey.

1

S ome families look forward to the month of June, which marks the beginning of the summer season, with its warm, lazy, sun-filled days at the Jersey shore. Others await December, which marks the winter season, with its festive holiday gatherings around the dinner table. September is never a favorite for children, because it means the end of summer vacation and the start of another school year. It is a time they must put away those sandy flip-flops in exchange for a pair of uncomfortable new shoes.

Scott Paterson, a tall, redheaded, freckle-faced seventh grader at Printab Academy in Verona, New Jersey, was a confirmed October enthusiast like the rest of his family. He loved the sound of the crunching leaves when he walked or jumped on them in the backyard, and he enjoyed seeing the colorful blanket they made on the lawn.

But most importantly, October meant Halloween. His parents, Ellen and Bobby, actually had a fetish for Halloween, going as far as to paint their colonial house orange, with black shutters and the front door black with orange trim, colors of the holiday that remained all year long. Their neighbors on Cypress Avenue called their house "the Halloween house," and the Patersons loved this nickname. Their attachment to

Halloween stemmed from the fact that Ellen and Bobby had met at a school dance on October 31, almost twenty years before. Just as some couples have their song, Ellen and Bobby, high school sweethearts, adopted Halloween as their holiday.

For the actual day, Bobby, an electrician and a kid at heart, wired his house so that when a visitor rang their front doorbell, it triggered a variety of eerie noises, a blast from a fog machine, and the recorded voices of Scott and his younger brother, Freddie, shrieking and yelling, "Help! Let me out! Save me!" with scary music echoing in the background. The reward for trick-or-treaters brave enough to enter the front door was an array of large cardboard cutouts of witches and goblins hanging in the foyer, swinging steadily with the help of a small ceiling fan.

Both boys looked forward to helping their dad with the wiring every year. Scott was especially interested in how things worked and loved working alongside and learning from his father in their home's basement workshop. Scott had just won first prize in the middle school's science fair; his entry was the robot they'd built together using snippets of wood, batteries, leftover wires, and a coat of blue paint. Ellen and Bobby were proud of Scott, the budding scientist, and had promised to take him to the Franklin Institute in Philadelphia during the next school vacation to experience its hands-on exhibits.

Fun-loving nine-year-old Freddie was more interested in building figurines with Legos. He spent a great deal of time in Scott's shadow. He looked up to his smart older brother and wanted to be involved in every aspect of Scott's life. Freddie was younger, but the brothers were often mistaken for twins; they had the same crooked smile and dimpled chin, the same red hair and freckles. While Bobby and Scott were creating their mechanical robot, Freddie did such a commendable job on his own robot—this one made of different shapes, colors, and sizes of Legos—that it was displayed on their fireplace mantel.

"Teach me how to make those noises that happen when the front door is opened," Scott insisted. "I want to try to do it myself; I think I can do it."

His dad patiently explained in a language that Scott understood.

"All right, we will practice during the year, and you will have your chance next Halloween," said Bobby, feeling pleased that his son shared his passion.

Scott's face broke into a smile of appreciation. His father answered the smile by saying, "Now I will have to change the wording on my truck to 'Paterson and Sons.'" He gave each of the boys a high five.

Their Halloween decorations had reached new heights this year, and Bobby added what became his favorite and most complicated feature: flashing orange and black lights that formed "Happy Halloween" on the Patersons' well-manicured front lawn. He was delighted when neighbors put notes saying "Nice work, Bob" in the orange-and-black mailbox secured to a wooden post cemented into the ground. He had wanted to do more and was encouraged by the mail, but Ellen had said, "Enough is enough! Soon the house will look ridiculous." With a big smile, she added her finishing touches of two pumpkins and two cornstalks on the front steps and went inside to relax before she started her annual pumpkin-cookie-baking ritual, wearing her orange-and-black apron tied around her petite waist. The expectant smell of Ellen's sugar cookies would gradually permeate the air.

"Just one more thing," said Bob as he turned to Scott. "How about giving your old man a hand stringing the lights on the roof?"

"Awesome," answered Scott, grateful for the opportunity

but surprised at the offer. "I would love it. Can we do it right now?"

"Sure," answered Bobby.

After Scott and Bobby took the old paint-speckled ladder from the garage and leaned it against the house, Bobby said, "Now, Scott, I'll be on the roof. You are not to go on the roof—do you understand? Your mother would kill me if I let you go up there. When you reach the top rung, you will hand me the lights that are in this blue canvas bag. Put it on your shoulder. Take it slowly—you'll be high. You're not afraid of heights, are you?"

"No, Dad, not that I know of. I can do it."

Bobby climbed the ladder, adjusted his glasses, and waited on the black asphalt-shingled roof. "Don't forget the bag with the lights. And, Freddie, you hold the ladder steady for your brother," Bobby shouted from the rooftop.

Scott cautiously started up the ladder, one rung at a time. He was a little nervous; his heart was beating rapidly, but he didn't want to let on. He felt like he was climbing Mount Everest. The top of the ladder looked so far away, and he was getting a little dizzy. But his dad was on the roof, smiling at him and encouraging him to continue.

"That's it, son. One rung at a time. Take your time."

The bag with the lights was weighing Scott's shoulder down and beginning to feel uncomfortable. He shifted the bag to the other shoulder, and the movement caused a feeling of dizziness that enveloped him. He lost his footing and slid down two or three rungs, dropping the bag of lights before trying to balance himself by holding on to the outside of the ladder.

Seeing him slip, Bobby, his heart pounding, sent his tall body zooming down the ladder to his boy. With every step down, Bobby's strong legs felt weaker and weaker until they began to shake him, not knowing in what condition he was going to find Scott.

Scott was halfway up the ladder before he tumbled to a grassy area on the ground. Though visibly shaken, he survived the fall with just a few scrapes and bruises and a damaged ego. Before Bobby could get a word out, Scott looked at his father, whose face had turned white, and said in a little voice, "I'm okay, Dad. I just got a little dizzy."

"Are you sure, son? I'm so angry at myself. That was so stupid of me. What if something had happened to you? I could never forgive myself. Just stay still for a few minutes. Do you need a doctor?" Tears rolled down Bobby's cheeks. He helped Scott stand up when he gave the thumbs up okay signal. Freddie, who had been holding the ladder, had gotten knocked down when Scott fell, so Bobby extended his strong hand to help his younger son as well.

"I'll be okay, Dad," stammered Scott. "I just need a Band-Aid for my knee. I guess I don't like heights."

When Scott and Freddie were up and off the ground, they gathered for a family hug.

"At Paterson and Sons, I'll be the designated electrician doing the ground work," Scott said with a chuckle.

Scott and Freddie got along very well together and felt that the best part of Halloween was going trick-or-treating from house to house as they carried oversize pillowcases taken from their parents' king-size bed. Whenever they saw their favorite candies, Kit Kats, 3 Musketeers, and Reese's Peanut Butter Cups, being dropped into their pillowcases, they gave each other a smile and a thumbs-up.

Upon returning home, the boys knew the first order of business was to empty all their candy on the living room carpet. Ellen would make sure they threw out any candy that was unwrapped or opened. Freddie counted his Kit Kats, Scott counted his Reese's Peanut Butter Cups, and when no one was looking Bobby managed to swipe all the 3 Musketeers. The rest of the candy went into a big glass cookie jar kept on a shelf in the pantry, which Ellen monitored to oversee how much candy they were eating each day.

Ellen enjoyed going to Dr. A's house. The neighborhood dentist liked to hand out plastic bags containing a toothbrush, a small tube of Colgate toothpaste, floss, and his business card. It was her favorite stop because she thought the items in the bags promoted a healthy mouth—and it was good advertising for her friend. "It would be great if he included a coupon for a free examination. I will have to mention that to him, and I want to be first," she said with a laugh.

The Mark's large house on the corner of Canterbury and Byron was the highlight for the boys. Mr. Mark owned a toy manufacturing company, and he arranged toys on Ping-Pong tables in his three-car garage. The older kids often changed their masks and returned several times to select different toys. They thought they were fooling Mr. Mark, but Mom assured Scott and Freddie that he knew what they were doing. "You know, Mr. Mark was a kid once. And, after all, it is Halloween."

Mrs. Lombardi, Ellen's good friend, was their last customary stop. When they got to her house, she had a hot cup of cocoa ready for them on her beige Formica kitchen table. "With marshmallows or without?" she would ask.

The boys found it odd that the cocoa was always hot and waiting for their arrival. They laughed when they pictured Mrs. Lombardi standing at the window all night, peeking behind her starched curtains and then taking the hot pot off the stove the moment she saw them walk to the door. Scott and Freddie really did not want the cocoa—they wanted to get home and check their haul—but they were polite. They drank their cocoa and tried to hurry Ellen along as she was gossiping with Mrs. Lombardi.

"Dad," said Scott one night as he was helping him finish hanging the Halloween characters in their front hall, "would you do me a favor?"

"Sure, son," he replied. "Just hand me the hammer. What is it?"

"Well, you know how Mom always walks around with Freddie and me on Halloween? Well, you know, I'm twelve years old now, and it is embarrassing. I am the only one of my friends who still has their mother trailing along. Everyone is going to make fun of me and call me a baby. It's bad enough that she questions all my friends when she gives them her homemade broken cookies in sandwich bags that are covered with alphabet stickers. She still thinks I am in nursery school. I want to go out alone this year. Can I?"

Bobby tried to keep a straight face, remembering feeling the same way as Scott felt when he was his age. "You know, Scott, your mom loves you and just wants to keep you safe."

"I know, Dad, but I want to go out with just my friends like the other kids."

"Okay, Scott. I will talk to Mom. Now let's get these goblins hung," replied Bobby.

2

This Halloween was going to be different; it was going to be extra special. Bobby had convinced Ellen to allow Scott to go trick-or-treating without her. "After all, Ellen, Scott will be twelve years old next month. Let him go with his friends. They stay in the neighborhood."

It was a big deal for Ellen. It meant that her child was growing up and didn't need his mother anymore.

For Scott, it was showing his independence.

After much discussion, Ellen suggested a compromise: Scott could go out without her and join his friends if they did not go beyond Grove Avenue and Bloomfield Avenue, was home by nine o'clock, and practiced his drums before he went out.

"Oh, thanks, Mom," Scott shouted while giving his father a thumbs-up and his mother a big hug. He ran up to his room to make a phone call in the privacy of his bedroom. When he contacted his friend, he told him to count him in for Halloween. Scott also urged him to find out if Rose from homeroom—who won second place in the science fair—was going to join the group. He liked her, but he was too shy to engage her in conversation in class. If she was with them that night, it would give him a chance to talk to her and discuss their science projects and maybe even arrange to work on one together. Perhaps, if the evening was developing smoothly, Scott might conjure up enough nerve to invite her to the Thanksgiving dance. Scott loved to dance and was light on his feet once the music started playing. He liked watching the hip-hop dancers on TV and picked up the moves very quickly. Many a night, he would be glued to the television while he watched *So You Think You Can Dance* and tried to perfect his break dancing.

When he heard Rose say she also liked Turkey Hill chocolate swirl ice cream—and could eat buckets of it right out of the container—he decided it could be an opening for him. Scott was pleased to have a plan.

On Halloween, Ellen always dressed up like a clown. This year Scott would not be embarrassed by his mother's yellow, green, and orange wig, red rubber nose, and old, stained tie.

Freddie would suffer, but he usually attempted to remain ten paces ahead so it looked like they were not together.

3

October 26, 2012

The Goldman family lived in Cedar Grove, New Jersey, the former home of the famous Meadowbrook Dinner Theater before it closed. David Goldman, the youngest member of the family was wearing his fuzzy Clifford costume and even though it was making him perspire he would not take it off. He wanted to eat his dinner in it, go to sleep in it, and even shower in it. He loved the feel of Clifford's soft red fur and kept massaging it with his small hands.

Dorothy smiled—showing an orthodontist's perfect creation—as she watched her son admiring himself in the front hall mirror. The costume was worth every penny; Dorothy had bought it at full price at the Halloween store. It was going to be a very special Halloween for David. Even though he was eight years old, this would be his first time trick-or-treating. She had promised him that they would drive past the well-known orange and black Halloween house in Verona, the next town, to see the light display on the front lawn. David had never been well enough to go out for Halloween because he was born with a serious heart condition. His parents generally worried that the weather was too cold, that his lips would turn blue, or that he would become too tired or sick. This year, Dr. Liz had said, "Bundle him up, put him in the stroller, and let him have some fun. He can walk to the front doors if there are not too many steps; otherwise, keep him in the stroller."

David was thrilled. This Halloween would be the best one yet. Most of his play was solitary, and it was not often that he had the opportunity to engage in fun activities like other kids.

His heart condition was called hypoplastic left heart syndrome. With HLHS, a rare congenital heart defect, the left ventricle of the heart was severely underdeveloped, affecting normal blood flow through the heart. Babies like David might not experience trouble for the first few days of life while the normal openings in the heart operate, but they quickly develop signs of cardiac failure after the openings close.

During his first week, David was healthy enough to have a bris, a Jewish tradition and commandment requiring a circumcision for Jewish boys on the eighth day. Many friends and relatives happily crowded into David's living room to attend this long-honored ceremony conducted by a mohel, the circumciser. At the conclusion of the ceremony, the chatty, hungry, and impatient guests gathered around the extended dining room table, which was set for a buffet lunch with fancy paper plates and shiny plastic silverware. The smorgasbord included bagels, salads, lox, whitefish, noodle puddings, and rugelach for dessert, enough for twice as many people that were there.

Shortly after the festivities, things took a turn for the worse. David developed a variety of breathing problems that caused his skin to turn blue. Even his little fingernails were blue. When he was given a bottle of warm formula, he did not possess the strength to drink it and simply fell asleep. He was not gaining weight, and it was then that he was given the affectionate nickname Bones that lasted his lifetime.

"Something is wrong," Dorothy said as she held her baby in her thin arms, trying in vain to feed him, and remembering how her older son had inhaled his bottle at the same age. "I think we better take him to the hospital," she said as her husband phoned the pediatrician.

Evan said, "Dr. Deb will meet us at the emergency room. Let's go."

The doctors examined David and ran a battery of tests, including a cardiogram and an echocardiogram. Dorothy and Evan waited almost an hour for the results in the crowded waiting room, flipping through old *People* magazines, nervously pacing the hospital's black and white floor, and calling family with updates on David and for checkups on Mark.

"What's taking them so long?" asked Dorothy. "He probably needs a diaper change and a bottle, and I have them both."

"Sit down. You are going to wear out the floor tiles. This is a hospital. The nurses have diapers and formula," Evan said as he helped her to a chair.

Finally, a young pediatric cardiologist appeared and invited them to his office. He had kind eyes, a soft voice, and an unhurried manner. "Your son's life is in danger. He suffers from a critical heart condition, hypoplastic left heart syndrome, and he needs an operation, which should be done immediately. If left untreated, the results are fatal."

Dorothy and Evan cried uncontrollably and asked the doctor to explain what was wrong several times before they understood what was going on with David.

Dorothy said, "Can we see him before you take him to the O.R.? I just want to see him and tell him that I love him.

He might be hungry or need his diaper changed. Everything is happening so quickly. I can't think."

"We will take care of all of that, Mrs. Goldman. I'll tell the nurses. Come this way to be with David before the surgery."

When they entered his room, their baby was surrounded by equipment and a host of medical staff in white coats. With the tubes and IVs, David looked so fragile and innocent.

The smell of alcohol made Dorothy feel lightheaded and nauseous. "Will he be all right? Please take good care of him." Tears ran down her moistened cheeks. "He's so little. He is not even seven pounds. How did this happen? I never even had a Diet Coke when I was pregnant. No one in our family has a bad heart. I followed all the instructions. I didn't do anything different this time than I did with Mark. I didn't feel any different. My obstetrician never said there was a problem, and he did plenty of tests. What happened?"

The cardiologist gently handed her a box of tissues and calmly and patiently explained that the causes for HLHS were unknown and that David's condition was not the fault of anyone. Her many questions centered around guilt and there were no explanations for them. It was heartbreaking for Dorothy and Evan.

David was closed up and full of tubes in an incubator. They held his bony hand through the round opening and remained with him until he was taken to the operating room.

This procedure would be the first of many. The Norwood procedure was a difficult operation that needed to be done by skilled surgeons. It created a new aorta, a blood vessel that carries oxygen rich blood from the left ventricle of the heart to the entire body, and kept him alive.

It was six weeks before he came home, and most of that time was on a respirator. David's older brother, five-year-old Mark, spent time with his grandparents and the extended family. The absence of his parents, who slept in David's hospital room on uncomfortable large chairs, was very difficult for him. Even though he was well cared for and enjoyed playing with his cousins, Isabel and Al, Mark wanted to go back to his own room with pictures of Derek Jeter on the wall and Yankee sheets on his bed.

Mark's kindergarten teacher assigned a parent-student project to the class. The challenge was to build a birdhouse out of any type of material. Evan was handy with tools and even had a well-supplied workshop in their basement with lots of extra wood. Mark's grandfather, Ben, was going to work with him since his dad was in the hospital with David. Ben was not as skilled as Evan in the handyman department, but he did his best with frequent calls to Evan for instruction and advice.

When they were almost finished, Mark started to cry and said, "I want my Daddy." There was no consoling him, and Evan was called home from the hospital to complete the task with his son. Mark needed that extra attention from his father.

David had another surgery that allowed him to breathe better, but it did not cure him. According to his doctors, his life was still in jeopardy.

"I don't believe David will crawl or walk," the cardiologist said.

All they heard was frightening and discouraging news from the medical team.

Dorothy asked her rabbi to say the beautiful and melodious Misheberach healing prayer for David every day at her synagogue. Dorothy was strong and optimistic." He will walk," she said. "He will get better. I have to believe that."

The day he came home was a joyous one, but it was a little scary for the family since they had to be David's nurses and medical staff. Many children with heart defects are prone to cognitive, physical, and language delays and have a lot of catching up to do. David required numerous therapists to help him develop properly. Physical therapists worked with him every day for years, coming to David's house to teach him how to crawl, how to walk, how to climb, and eventually how to run. Speech therapists also spent many years teaching him how to talk, which he accomplished at the age of four. David was not allowed to attend school during the early formative times because of the potential germs and his low stamina. As he got older, he was home-schooled by teachers from the public school system, and he looked forward to their weekly visits to his playroom and the little surprises he was allowed to pick from the surprise box they brought with them. The school was wonderful to David and the family, even arranging Skype sessions so he and the children had an opportunity to get to know one another.

Friends and family started to refer to David as the miracle baby. All the years of work that the doctors, teachers, therapists, and family had spent on David's recovery were coming to fruition. He was beating the odds, and to the amazement of the medical community, he was walking and talking.

4

During the first few years of David's life, it would have been very dangerous if he had caught a cold or gotten sick. Whenever Mark came home from school, he immediately washed his hands at the kitchen sink, and whenever a playdate was arranged, it was always scheduled at his friend's house, provided his friend was healthy. No guests—adults or children—were allowed in the Goldman home. Purell was positioned on every sink and every countertop.

David followed a daily routine of medicines and therapies. A good part of his day was spent enjoying music on his portable CD player or watching TV. He loved watching Thomas The Train and tried to say the names of his favorite train characters, Thomas and Percy. This was done by indicating their numbers with his hand. One finger meant blue Thomas and six fingers were for green Percy. He communicated in this way when he played. He became a *Thomas the Train* expert and knew the numbers on every train.

Dorothy spent hours each day on the beige carpeted floor talking and building train tracks with David. He gleefully pushed and pulled the wooden trains through tunnels and up and down hills. For her, life did not exist outside her house or outside the train's roundhouse that monopolized most of the playroom floor.

When David turned seven, his doctors at the Miriam Irving Memorial Hospital thought it was time to place David on the heart transplant waiting list because his heart was too damaged and weak to pump enough blood through his growing body. He could not survive much longer with his own heart.

Dorothy said, "A heart transplant is surgery that will remove your sick heart and replace it with a healthy one from a deceased person. The person who gives you that heart is called a donor."

"Yuck. I don't want a dead person's heart. Whose heart am I going to get? How did the donor die? Who is going to die?"

"We don't know," said Dorothy.

"Will it be next week?" David interjected.

"Probably not," answered his mom. "Your name goes on a waiting list, and it might take six months to a year before it's your turn."

"That's a long time to wait. Where do we wait—in a waiting room? How will we know when it's my turn?" asked David. "Will we need a number like in Caputo's Bakery?"

"Dr. Liz knows our phone number. When it's time, she will call us on my cell phone. We might be at home, in the car, or even playing Uno in the backyard. We will have to go to the hospital immediately to get your new heart," Dorothy said with a nervous laugh. "Dr. Liz told me to keep my cell phone out all the time and not to turn it off when I go to sleep. She might call during the day or night."

"What will happen to my old heart? Will I have two hearts? Where will they put it?"

"It might be used for testing," Dorothy replied without hesitation. "Nobody else will get it, and it won't be in your body anymore. You will only have one heart; the brand-new one will go in your chest to replace the old one. You will have a scar on your chest where the old one was removed and the new one was placed. Many people have the same scars to show that they also had heart surgery." Dorothy lifted David's Giants T-shirt and traced a line on his veiny chest.

"Is it like a heart tattoo?" asked David.

Dorothy smiled and said, "That's a good way of explaining it: a heart tattoo. I like that. I'll have to remember those words and tell it to Dr. Liz. She might use that expression with her other patients."

"Will it hurt when they take out my old heart?" David asked.

"You will be asleep when they take out your old heart, and when you wake up, you will have the new heart and your heart tattoo on your chest," said Dorothy.

"Can I play ball when I get my new heart and be on a team with a uniform that says my name on the back of the jersey?"

"Sure, you can. You can do anything the other kids do. You can even go to school. I will buy you your very own Giants backpack, and you can pick out any lunchbox that you want at Toys R Us. And guess what? You won't have to go in the stroller when we go out—you can walk. You will have a healthy heart. You will be new."

"I want to play ball like my brother."

5

Weather Report for October 28, 2012

"**B**oys, come and see the weather report on the TV," Ellen Paterson said. "It doesn't look good for Halloween."

"Don't tell us that," said the boys as they plopped themselves down on the comfortable couch.

"Feet off the table, boys," said Ellen while pushing their legs off the glass coffee table.

"This is the report from the National Weather Service: dangerous Hurricane Sandy to hit the Northeast," the reporter said. "Good evening. Dangerous Hurricane or Superstorm Sandy swept across the Bahamas and is now upgraded from a tropical storm to a category 1 hurricane. It is expected to strike New Jersey on October 29 with winds of eighty miles per hour. Stay inside, possible power outage is expected. Be prepared and locate your flashlights and batteries. High winds and drenching rain is forecasted. Beware of falling trees and branches. This could be the largest tropical storm in the Atlantic. Stay tuned for updates on Hurricane Sandy."

"This sounds like a big one. I'll get our candles ready. Boys, do you know where the flashlights are in case our power goes out?"

"It will probably be nothing. The weather reports always hype everything up, and they close the schools. Everyone gets excited and runs to ShopRite, and then there is no storm—just empty grocery shelves. But, just in case, the flashlights are in the kitchen cabinet next to the dish towels." Scott went back to playing Sudoku on his iPhone.

"They are interviewing Governor Christie on the television now," said Ellen. "He said that if the storm is as bad as it is forecasted, he is going to cancel Halloween. He doesn't want the kids walking in the street with downed wires and fallen branches."

"Just my luck," said Scott. "This was going to be a special Halloween for me. Oh, please don't let that happen. I've been looking forward to it."

"Scott has a girlfriend. I heard you talking on the phone," said Freddie teasing Scott in a singsong manner. "Scott has a girlfriend. Scott has a girlfriend."

"Stop it. I do not—and don't listen to my phone calls, you jerk," Scott said.

"There is nothing to do except wait," said Scott's mom as she continued to watch the broadcast.

That night, Ellen could hear the wind howling against the house. When she put the outside lights on, she could see the big oak trees swaying back and forth.

"It's bad out there," said Bob Paterson when he came home with his hair looking like it was in an electric socket. "I was almost blown away. It took all my strength to get back into the house. I hope you don't have plans for tonight. Nobody is going out."

"We have a history test tomorrow, and I was going to go next door for a study group that is meeting there."

"Don't go!" said Dad. "There probably will be no school."

"Yeah!" shouted the boys.

The lights in the house started to flicker.

"Get the flashlights," called Ellen. "The lights might go out."

"The lights just went off in my room. It is completely dark up there, and the TV just went off. I need a flashlight now," Freddie said as he walked slowly down the dark stairs.

"I need a flashlight to finish my Sudoku puzzle," Scott said.

"We are having a storm, and all you can think of is your stupid Sudoku? Give it a break," Freddie said as he looked for a flashlight.

"See if the phone works," Dad said. "Pick it up. Is there a dial tone?"

"No dial tone, Dad. I hope Grandma is okay."

Dad said, "She'll be fine. The care center is prepared for emergencies like this. This is exactly why she is there—so we wouldn't have to worry in these types of emergencies. We can use our cell phone to check on her. Give her a call, Ellen, but make it quick. The phone is not fully charged.

As the night progressed, the storm got worse. The house got darker and colder because they had no power, no lights, and no heat. The wind was blowing fiercely, and the big branches were falling from the trees and bouncing off the house. The roof sounded like it was cracking.

The family sprawled out on the cold living room floor with their Eveready flashlight to play Monopoly, bundled up in their winter jackets and knitted hats and gloves. Dinner was peanut-butter-and-grape-jelly sandwiches on soft white bread. What a treat! But even wrapped up in heavy camp blankets, the family was cold. It was getting to be no fun anymore, and they were uncomfortable. Even creating a party atmosphere by eating bags of curly potato chips and drinking cherry cokes did not make them happy. Still wearing their down jackets and wool hats, they took their heavy blankets and went to bed listening to the whistling wind banging the unhinged shutters against the house, which reminded Ellen and Bob that they never got the shutters fixed. Bang, bang, bang.

The next morning, the power was still out. The house was even colder; even the walls felt cold. The yard was filled with fallen branches and rain-soaked maple and oak leaves.

Bob listened to the news on his iPhone and discovered that the airports were closed. Many streets were so badly flooded that residents and their pets were being rescued from their homes in rowboats. "I guess we are not in such bad shape compared to other areas," he said.

"Look outside," Freddie said.

"Oh my goodness," Ellen exclaimed as she looked out the window.

A huge oak tree in the front yard was uprooted, displaying all of its roots and leaving a tremendous crater in the ground. Its branches were entangled in an electric line that was attached to the house. The tree looked precarious as it swayed back and forth in the strong wind. It was barely being held up as it leaned on a branch from another big oak tree. It reminded Ellen of a loose tooth that was waiting to come out with one tug. The giant oak was swaying back and forth and moving to and fro with the quick rhythm of the screeching wind.

"If that tree falls the wrong way, it could hit our roof," Ellen said. "Isn't that the gigantic tree that the tree guy was supposed to cut down last summer?"

"Let me see. I want to see." Scott raced through the living room.

The front door opened and slammed shut, taking everyone by surprise.

"Where is Scott going? Scott!" Ellen dashed to the living room window to watch the swinging tree.

The wind blew Scott closer and closer to the giant leafy oak.

"Bob, tell him to come in. It's too dangerous out there! That tree is being held up by one branch! It is going to fall soon with this heavy wind and drenching rain. My cell phone just beeped issuing a warning to beware of trees that are still filled with leaves because with the strength of this wind, they topple more readily. In big letters it said that residents should stay inside. What's the matter with that kid? For a smart kid, he's awfully stupid." Ellen bolted to the front door and was met with a strong gust of wind when she pulled it open. "Bob, come quickly. The wind has slammed Scott against the tree! The supporting branch is breaking. Scott is in trouble, he can't move. Scott, watch out!

"Mom, Dad, Freddie, ANYBODY, wailed Scott."

> "The tree… the tree. Watch out. Watch
> out. Help. Help! Oh no! My baby, my baby,
> shrieked Ellen."

Crack! Bang!

"Scott! Scott, Ellen screamed." But it was too late. The giant oak had fallen and took Scott with it.

The world went silent except for the terrifying sound of ambulance sirens that filled the neighborhood.

6

The call came when David was still prancing around in his Clifford costume and beginning to make an attempt to get ready for bed. Hurricane Sandy had spared his neighborhood in Cedar Grove. Although it was just fifteen minutes away from all the damage in Verona, their house never lost power. Friends had come to their house during the day to charge their phones—using every available outlet—and keep warm. Those with charged cell phones contacted Public Service to get an idea of how long the power outage would last. Public Service wasn't definite in their response, but they estimated several days to a week. People who were lucky enough to get a room checked into the Holiday Inn and Marriott to keep warm, take a hot shower, and let the kids watch TV. It was a bonanza for the hotels in the areas that had power.

Evan put a sign "warming station" on the door of their large colonial house. It was a very busy and social day in their home with lots of people coming and going, chatting, and sitting around their rustic, farm-style kitchen with steaming coffee and hot cocoa being made every hour. Their friends were delighted that they had a warm place for the kids to play and keep out of their hair, while they had a chance to get together and talk about the power outage.

It was past Mark and David's bedtime when everyone finally left.

Dorothy's cell phone rang.

"Hello, Dorothy. This is Dr. Liz. We have a heart for David."

"What?"

"Oh my G-d. You're kidding!" Dorothy was crying and screaming at the same time. "I can't believe it. Tell me this is for real."

"It's for real," answered Dr. Liz. "Have him at the hospital in four hours. The heart has been checked out, and it's perfect for David. We are sending a doctor and staff to retrieve it now for our little guy. If all goes well, he will have a new heart by sometime tomorrow. He should be in the hospital for about three to six weeks. Meet me on the cardiac floor. We will be looking for you. Give David a big hug and kiss for me."

Dorothy stood in the middle of the kitchen and said, "Evan that was Dr. Liz on the phone. They have a heart for David!"

Everyone started to cry and hug one another in disbelief.

Dorothy squeezed David, hugged him, and twirled him around the kitchen. Her tears were wetting both their cheeks. "You are going to have a healthy heart," she screamed as loud as she could.

Everyone pulled themselves together after reacting to the joyous news and realized it was really going to happen.

"We have to pack your suitcase. We certainly don't want to be late for this party," said Dorothy.

David said, "Can I bring my Madagascar and Daddy Camp videos and my stuffed bear and lion on my bed? What about Connect Four and my blanket? Oh, and a deck of cards?"

"You can bring them all," answered Dorothy.

Uncle Dan, Aunt Nancy, Isabel, Alec, and the grandparents arrived at their house with big smiles to hug David and support the family, although their eyes showed concern. They brought a bottle of vintage champagne to toast David.

"I've been saving this bottle for a special occasion, and this certainly is one. I'll get out the glasses." David's grandfather reached for a stack of Dixie paper cups.

"No paper cups for this toast. This calls for our good glassware," Dorothy said as she lined up her Waterford on the counter.

"L'Chaim, good health to David," they shouted and clicked their glasses when the cork popped, spilling some champagne on the counter.

"Papa, I'm going to play basketball," David said when he saw his grandfather.

"Yes, you are, my buddy—and we will be there to watch you," Papa said with tears in his eyes as he lifted David into his arms for a long hug.

The family was overwhelmed with happiness, but they were also apprehensive about the surgery, the recovery, and the unknown, which included a lifetime of antirejection drugs. This was virgin territory for them. A heart transplant sounded like something from *Star Wars*.

Mark was going to go home with his grandparents. Even though he was not the patient, the situation was very difficult for him. He needed lots of hugs and kisses. As David's older brother, there were many times that he took on the role of parent and caregiver. He had become a worrier and a little lonely even though the time separated from his parents couldn't be helped. David's family was so excited, but they looked at each other in utter disbelief.

"Let's make this a total party," Dorothy said. "I don't know a better way to celebrate than with ice cream. Ice cream for everyone." She went to the freezer to take out David's favorite, Turkey Hill Rocky Road ice cream." David, you can't eat anything after ten o'clock, so come have a little now."

They had waited eight years, since the day he was born, with six agonizing but hopeful months on the transplant list for David to get a healthy heart. It was what they wished and prayed for, but David getting a new heart meant a family gathered somewhere was not celebrating. They were mourning the loss of their child. The Goldman family was aware of the protocol that the recipient of the heart wouldn't learn the name of the donor until a year later if the donor agreed to reveal it.

When one door closes, another one opens, Dorothy thought.

The family packed their suitcases, and David packed as if he were going on a vacation, bringing toys and videos. In preparation for David's hospital stay, his parents surprised him with his own iPad, which added to his celebratory mood.

"Can I wear my Clifford costume to the hospital and show Dr. Liz?"

"You sure can," his parents answered.

David and his parents quickly packed up their SUV, which was filled with the familiar smell of Dorothy's perfume, got Mark ready to go with his grandparents, and prepared to leave for the hospital amid hugs, kisses, and tears.

"Good luck! We love you."

"I'm getting a new heart."

"Mark, have a good time with Grandma and Papa," Dorothy shouted as the SUV started down the driveway, "We'll call you, and be good."

"Wait a minute. Stop the car. Open the window, "yelled Mark as he was running down the driveway following the car. Mark handed David a photo of the two of them building a giant sandcastle on the beach that he had taken from his dresser. "This is for you, Bones. Good luck."

"Thanks Mark. I love you."

The two brothers embraced and high-fived through the open window.

Dorothy had a lump in her throat thinking about her boys and their unusual and wonderful bond.

On the pediatric cardiac floor, Dr. Liz greeted them with hugs. She was already in her scrubs. "The heart is here. We are getting ready for you. How do you feel, David?"

"Okay."

"Are you ready to go?"

"Not really, Dr. Liz," David said. "There is something that I am really scared about. I have a question for you."

"Okay. Let's talk about it." Dr. Liz pulled out chairs for all of them. She wanted to give David as much time as he needed for his questions before he went into surgery.

Dorothy and Evan never heard him mention that he was scared, although they knew that it was more than normal. They were pleased that he was going to express his fears.

"What am I going to look like with my new heart?"

Dr. Liz started to get technical, explaining about the scar and the other incisions until David interrupted her.

"My Mom told me about that. I mean my face."

"Your face?" Dr. Liz said.

"Yes, my face. Will I have a different face? Will I have my donor's face? What if the donor is a girl? Will I have a girl's face? How will people recognize me?" Tears started to roll down David's cheeks.

When Dorothy heard the question, she wanted to wrap her arms around David, hug him, and protect him by smothering her baby with kisses. But she didn't. David asked Dr. Liz the question, so she was going to let her handle it.

Dr. Liz took David into her private office, closed the door, and took out a book with pictures of a heart transplant. She showed David that the heart was the only organ in his body that was going to be touched. Everything else would remain the same. After that, she explained that the only connection that the hospital and doctors have with the donor is the specific organ that is being transplanted. The transplant team never saw the person, and the organ arrived in a small medical kit. "Only that organ was taken out of the donor's body and will be put into your body. So, you have nothing to be worried about. When you wake up, you will still have your handsome face, those big brown eyes with their long eye lashes, and your gorgeous smile. You will be the same David as you are right this minute except you will be healthier and stronger." She wrapped her arms around him.

"Thanks, Dr. Liz. I feel better now."

"Your mom and dad are in the waiting room. Go out and tell them that we straightened everything out, and then I will take you to the operating room to get you ready." Dr. Liz opened her office door and gave Dorothy and Evan a big smile.

They mouthed a thank you and blew her a kiss.

It was time to prep David.

Dorothy and Evan were very nervous and very teary as they waited in the spacious lounge. The thought of taking out David's heart and replacing it with a new, healthy, beating heart was amazing and frightening. They were knowledgeable about the procedure and the risks. They knew most of the doctors and nurses on the cardiac floor because they had been frequent visitors for eight years. The doctors and nurses on Dr. Liz's team were on first-name basis with the Goldman family. All of them knew and loved David and made a special effort to greet Dorothy and Evan to assure them that their son would be well taken care of.

"Why don't you go down to the cafeteria to get a cup of coffee? You probably could use it after that incident," Dr. Liz said. "It's going to be many hours. It will take several hours just to finish prepping him. He is doing fine, and we will keep you informed."

Dorothy did not want to leave the lounge, but Evan offered to get the coffee. "Keep an eye on my laptop. I'm leaving it on the chair. Do you want anything with the coffee—a muffin or a cheese Danish?"

"No, thanks. I can't eat now. I don't think anything will go down." She twirled her long brown hair and yawned, which she did when she was nervous.

After he left, she noticed a couple in the corner of the lounge. They were about her age, and the man had his arm around the woman's shoulder. The woman seemed to be having trouble catching her breath.

"Just take a deep breath, Mrs. Paterson," said the doctor who was holding her hand.

The doctor escorted them toward the door. At that point the sad man turned, looked at Dorothy and whispered, "What brings you here?"

"My son is in surgery."

"You have a son? How old is he?" said the man in a quiet, shaky voice.

"Eight," Dorothy replied. "I have two sons. What brings you here?"

"Bob, this is not the time to be social. Come on." Ellen tugged on his sleeve as the tears rolled down her face.

The man clutched his sobbing wife's hand and started to leave the lounge. He abruptly stopped and said stammering, "Our son died today, our oldest. We had two sons. Now we only have our Freddie. I can't believe these words are coming out of my mouth. Maybe I am having a nightmare. Someone wake me up and say the nightmare went away." He closed his eyes, pursed his lips, and shook his head as his sad eyes filled with tears.

"Oh, I'm so sorry." Dorothy stood up holding on to her chair. "Is there anything I can do for you?"

"It's too late! Good luck to your boy." He turned to his wife and said, "I'm sorry, honey. I thought the hurt would disappear if I acted normal, but it didn't. I guess it is time for us to go, time to leave Scott. "Weeping and holding each other up for support they slowly left.

Watching them go made Dorothy feel as if there was no air left in the room.

At that moment, one of the nurses peeked into the room and said, "We haven't begun yet. We are still prepping."

Dorothy felt dizzy. She sat down, moved the computer, put her head in her arms, and wept, allowing fortune to shine on her.

7

T he very worst thing that can happen to parents is to lose a child—it is an incomparable tragedy—but losing a child suddenly and without any warning of the death is worse than terrible. It doesn't give your mind or body any preparation. There are no goodbyes, no expressions of love, no words, no hugs, no kisses or holding one another, and no opportunities to fill the child's final bucket list.

Scott's death was shattering to Bobby and Ellen Paterson and their youngest son, Freddie. When the white gleaming ambulance with its siren and flashing blue and red lights took Scott away, it was an out-of-body experience for them. They felt like they were watching a frightening medical TV program that they couldn't turn off regardless of how hard they tried. It felt like it was happening to someone else. One minute, they were preparing for Halloween—happily hanging goblins and witches—and the next minute, they were preparing for a funeral.

It was not the proper order of life for a child to die before the parents. They were filled with anger, grief, and guilt. Ellen and Bob couldn't face a public funeral with their friends bringing their children who were alive and well when Scott was gone. So, they decided to have a gravesite service just for the family. They didn't want to listen to everyone telling them how sorry they were or listen to them complaining about their busy schedules of dropping off and picking up their kids for school and soccer practice. How lucky they were to have only that to worry about. The scars were too new and too raw. It was too soon, too difficult. How could they go on living? It was hard enough to get up in the morning, pull up the white, fringed bedroom shade, and get through another day. When they saw Scott's empty bed with the bedspread neatly tucked under the mattress, probably fixed by Aunt Molly, it was as heart-wrenching as it was to watch Freddie walking aimlessly from his room to Scott's over and over again. They longed to see the bedspread piled in a heap on the floor with Scott's dirty socks and underwear on top of it. The smell of his hair gel still lingered on his pillow.

They tried hard to be understanding and answer Freddie's many questions about death.

When they called Pastor Daniel Benn to tell him about Scott's passing, they told him the difficulty they were having answering Freddie's questions about his brother's demise. Pastor Dan, as he liked to be called, came over immediately. The shattered family needed much comfort as they dealt with Scott's senseless death. He tried his best to give them the care and support they needed and to familiarize them with the format of a Christian funeral. The family decided against a church service, against an open casket, against music, against flowers, and against a eulogy. At that time, all they could handle or think about was a quick graveside service.

A black limousine that the funeral director sent was waiting at the curb, with its driver, when they opened their front door the next morning to go to the cemetery.

"I'm not going in that car. You can't make me. Let's take our own car," Ellen said.

"Okay, honey. We'll go in our own car." Bob was bent over like an old man.

Freddie was carrying a big plastic garbage bag.

"What's in the bag, Freddie?" Bobby asked.

"It's the robot you built with Scott. He was so proud of it. I think he will want to keep it with him."

Bobby and Ellen looked at Freddie and looked at each other with tears in their eyes. They couldn't say a word. They couldn't do anything but hold him and kiss him.

Bobby said, "I'll give it to Pastor Dan. He'll make sure that Scott gets it."

The cemetery was empty on that brisk fall day except for a few visitors bringing pots of yellow and white mums to the marble and stone graves of their departed loved ones. Some of the bushes had storm-soaked toilet paper wrapped around them, a reminder of the Halloween that never happened.

Pastor Dan guided them to straight-backed chairs near the gravesite. The muscles in their faces were clenched as they took their seats. Their heads were bent, and their knuckles were white from the pressure of holding on to one another as they gazed at the mound of fresh dirt.

Pastor Dan said, "We are gathered here to say farewell to Scott Paterson and commit him to the hands of God."

It was a shock to every nerve in their bodies when they saw the gravediggers continuing to prepare the ground for the coffin. The time had come to say their final goodbye to Scott.

Ellen screamed frantically when the gravediggers began to lower the solid mahogany coffin into its final resting place. She tried to prevent it from happening by attacking the workers.

Bob had to pull her off a man's leg while she was kicking and wailing. "No, no, Scott, Scott … not yet. We have so many more things to do and say, we have to take you to the Franklin Institute. I love I love you."

She finally wore herself out and collapsed in Bobby's arms.

Bobby and Pastor Dan carried Ellen to the car, and the exhausted family headed home—minus one son.

S ince his transplant, David was beginning to lead a life that had never seemed possible. After spending several weeks recuperating in the hospital plus many months recuperating at home and getting accustomed to the rhythm of his new heart, he slowly began a normal life of adjusting to going out and being with other people. His team of transplant doctors presented him with a plan that involved frequent medical checkups and weekly heart biopsies immediately after the transplant and then not so frequently as time passed. The visits showed whether his body was rejecting his new heart. Fortunately, the new heart was doing just fine. The checkups also included EKGs, blood tests, and pulmonary reviews. He never complained and always rolled with the punches. David received an NFL watch with an alarm, a Velcro band, and a big Giants logo. It would ring every morning and evening at nine o'clock, signaling that it is was time to take his antirejection drugs.

For the first few months, David was required to wear a white gauze mask when he was in a crowd. He didn't mind it or feel embarrassed by it. The choice was to wear a mask or stay home, and he chose the mask every time. He had heard about people getting very sick after a transplant, and he didn't want to be one of them.

His doctors were thrilled with his recovery. David was right on schedule with every aspect of the process. Medically, he was their poster child.

His first time out in a large group was a party for transplant patients at the hospital. Dorothy told him that he didn't have to wear a mask because the hospital was very careful about germs. When David saw all the people in the room, some still with IV tubes and masks, he panicked. He wouldn't go into the room without a mask, and he started to cry. "I'm not going in. I want a mask. I'm going to get sick. I don't want to go back to the hospital."

The medical mask had become part of him, and it was his security blanket.

The doctors from the transplant team tried to assure him that it was all right and that he was not in danger at the sterile hospital.

Dorothy realized there was so much fear of getting sick bottled up in that little brain of his that no one was addressing. Finally, a mask was found because he was so distraught.

David joined the party and felt safe.

Dorothy made a mental note to start weaning David off the mask now that he was getting better.

A boy in a wheelchair who was not much older than David was also wearing a mask. They started talking, and David learned that he had a diseased kidney and was waiting for a transplant. He had been waiting six months and had been put in the hospital a week earlier because he couldn't manage at home anymore. The boy was praying that he would get a healthy kidney before it was too late.

I'm such a lucky kid, thought David.

That summer, the doctors gave David permission to go

without the mask if he was in a healthy environment and David felt secure enough to do so.

David and his family took frequent trips to the beach that summer. When they were on the beach, Dorothy didn't want David to take off his swim shirt. David's scar—or his "heart tattoo" was still raw and red. Dorothy worried that he would be embarrassed when others saw it. She told him the truth that a new scar shouldn't be exposed to the sun, but that was not her real reason.

David kept asking to remove his shirt. He did not care at all about his scar.

One day, they were talking to Sam, a young, muscular lifeguard who knew about David's heart transplant. He picked up his shirt to reveal a scar on his sunburned, well-oiled chest and said, "Look, buddy. We are in the same club. We have matching scars. That makes us brothers for life."

David still had a lot of convincing to do before Dorothy would allow him to expose his chest—even with the help of his new lifeguard pal. More and more, she was realizing that he was a self-assured young boy. Perhaps she didn't give him enough credit.

A trip to Jenkinson's Amusement Park in Seaside Park, which was up and running after being badly damaged by Hurricane Sandy, was part of the family excursion to the beach. It smelled like hot dogs, sauerkraut, and cotton candy. There were many games to play and various sizes of stuffed dogs, monkeys, and giraffes to win. The lines for the rides were long with whining kids and impatient parents.

When Mark saw the Ferris wheel, he said, "Come on, David. Let's go on the Ferris wheel. We can sit together. It's so much fun,"

"I'm not going on that Ferris wheel. Don't even think about it. I'm afraid of heights," David said.

"I don't think you have ever had the experience of being on a Ferris wheel or anything else of considerable height," said Dorothy.

"I just know that I am afraid of heights. I remember being afraid of heights, and I'm not going," David said. "I am going to get dizzy when I look down like that time I was on the roof, and I might even fall off the Ferris wheel."

Dorothy said, "On the roof? You were never on the roof. Are you kidding? I would never let you go on the roof. You probably dreamt it. I think you are imagining something and being silly. You can't fall off the Ferris wheel. You are strapped in very tightly. I'm not even sure you should be going on a Ferris wheel yet. There's no point in even discussing it. Let's do something else while Mark goes on the ride. We'll try to win a prize, a stuffed animal, or a bag of Bazooka bubble gum by knocking down the bowling pins."

"After that, I want to play the game with the water pistol. They have the best prizes. I saw a kid win a blow-up baseball player," said David.

Many of the rides required a certain height, and David waited every time to be measured to see if he was finally eligible. His damaged heart that he lived with for so many years didn't allow him to grow at a normal rate. He tried his best to talk his way onto the rides by schmoozing with the attending college kid. He was a good small talker, especially about football, but it didn't work. He would have to wait another season to go on the rides.

He loved the summer with the freedom of the beach, the sounds and smell of the ocean, and the chance to go places with his family.

To everyone's dismay, David developed an uncharacteristic phobia of rainstorms, thunder, and the dark. At one point, he got so anxious during a summer storm that he wouldn't go outside to get into the car to go shopping with his mom. He also had frequent nightmares and woke up screaming and crying in the middle of the night. When his parents went into his room, he would be tossing and turning and trying to hide under his blankets. David's dark hair and face were soaking wet from perspiration and needed to be washed with a washcloth.

Dorothy would get into his twin bed with him to calm him down and rub his back like she did when he was an infant.

It took a couple of the episodes before he was able to verbalize what was frightening him.

"The sky is so dark, and something is going to fall on my head," he said repeatedly.

"What is going to fall on your head?" his mom and dad asked.

"I don't know," he stammered with the pillow over his head. "But it is big and scary."

Dorothy and Evan decided to put a nightlight in his room, and it seemed to make a difference. Eventually, the nightmares stopped, but he continued to be bothered by storms. When Dorothy consulted, his pediatrician, she was told that children frequently develop fears and they would pass as quickly as they appeared. The doctor didn't seem concerned about them.

Dorothy thought there was more to it than that, but she couldn't quite put her finger on it. She wondered if he was remembering Hurricane Sandy and the fallen trees all over town. She felt better after she correlated his fears with the storm. Basically, David was not a fearful child. Something else might be going on in his head.

9

After the summer, David started school for the first time. Dorothy drove him to school every morning and watched him climb the large cement steps with a determined swagger as if the day was waiting just for him. He walked to the entrance wearing his Giants backpack without too much trouble and always turned around and gave a quick wave goodbye. He loved school and making friends on his own. The children in his class were dumbfounded when they heard he had gotten a new heart.

"You can't get a new heart," one child said during lunch. "You already have one. Don't tell a lie. There is no such a thing as a heart store. Where do you get a new heart?"

"Someone gave me his heart, a dead person," answered David.

"Now I know you are lying," answered his laughing classmate.

"I got a transplant. I'm not lying." He lifted his shirt above the scar that covered most of his skinny chest.

"Wow," he said. "My brother has a scar on his knee from when he cut himself, but yours is much bigger. Can I touch it?"

"Sure," said David enjoying the positive attention.

Another boy walked over to their table to see what was happening. "What are you looking at?"

"David had a transplant," he answered as if he was an expert on the subject.

"What's a transplant?"

"You know, you get it from a dead person."

"Oh, is it catching? My mother said not to get sick before my cousin's wedding."

"No, it's not catching." David suppressed a laugh.

"Okay. Can I have some of your pretzels?"

"Sure," David said. "Take the whole bag. I'm full."

That was the end of the transplant talk. The boys took out their baseball and hockey trading cards, and the conversation turned to sports. David didn't have any cards, but he was delighted to be part of the fun. He was going to ask Dorothy to get him some cards after school.

One of the first highlights as a result of his transplant came when he was invited to a classmate's birthday party. He had never attended a nonfamily party, and he was overjoyed to be part of it. The invitation arrived in the mail with a picture of a soccer ball on the stamp.

"David, you have a letter," called Mom.

"Me?"

"Yes, you."

"Who is it from?"

"Open it up and see." She handed him the letter.

He hurriedly tore open the envelope and handed it back to his mother to read.

"It's an invitation to Louie's birthday party." She thought it might be a soccer party and immediately started to worry. David was not allowed to engage in contact sports yet, and it would be difficult to have to decline his very first invitation. Thankfully, the invitation did not mention any sports.

"For me?"

"Yes, it's for you."

"Can I go?" David smiled and crossed his fingers.

"I don't see why not," she replied.

"Is that a yes or a no?"

"It's a yes, you silly goose."

David jumped up and down and hugged his mom. "I am so excited. I want to be the first one at Louie's house. When is it?"

"Next weekend. You can be the first one there."

"And don't come in like I am a baby. Drop me off."

"Okay." She was smiling from ear to ear; her little boy was going to a birthday party just like any other kid. "I'll give you a small bottle of Purell to keep in your pocket. Don't forget to use it before and after you eat."

David was at the birthday party only a short time before Dorothy received a text from Louie's mother. Thoughts started to whirl through her mind when she saw the message. She went over the possibilities in her head. "Hi, Dorothy. Please call me. David is fine."

Dorothy immediately picked up the phone. "Hi, Mary. Is David okay? What's going on?"

"David is okay," replied Mary. "The birthday boy loves Chinese food, and as a surprise, we had a caterer bring in a Chinese buffet for the kids. We thought it would be a nice change from the pizza that they get at every party. Louie was thrilled when he saw his favorite foods—spareribs, fried rice, and General Tso's chicken—but when David saw the buffet, he got upset."

A sense of relief ran through Dorothy's thin body. "Say no more. This is what happened. David is not allowed to eat from a buffet because of his compromised immune system. Is he crying?"

"I'm so sorry, Dorothy. I didn't know. No, he's not crying. He just won't eat anything."

"Do you have any turkey in the house?"

"Yes," answered Mary. "I just bought some at the ShopRite today. It's Boar's Head."

"Good. Can you make him a turkey sandwich on rye if you have it—and with nothing on the bread? He will eat that."

"Sure."

"Thanks so much, Mary. I am sorry to trouble you. Can I speak to David—and wish Louie a happy birthday for me."

As soon as David heard Dorothy's voice, he started to cry. "Everything is okay, David. Take a deep breath and calm down. You did the right thing by not eating from the buffet. I am so proud of you. You acted like a big boy. You were responsible."

"I was afraid I was going to get sick," David said through his tears.

"No, you are not going to get sick. You did the right thing. You didn't eat anything wrong. Do you want me to pick you up now—or do you want to stay?"

"I want to stay," said David. "I'm having fun."

"Okay. Louie's mother is going to make you a turkey sandwich. You can eat it. I will pick you up when the party is over. I love you. Have a good time."

"Bye, Mom. Can I have a piece of the birthday cake?"

"Of course."

"What about the ice cream?"

"Sure. Maybe they have Turkey Hill Rocky Road. I know you love that."

Dorothy was so proud of the way he was able to say no to the Chinese buffet and not be influenced by his peers on his first excursion out of the house without her. *He will be all right in this world as long as modern medicine stays ahead of him. He was born with confidence.*

10

The year after Scott's death passed slowly for the Patersons. To mark the year, they had a small memorial service for their close friends and a few of Scott's friends. The twelve months had been somewhat of a healer, but the hole in their hearts would never disappear. Freddie had become an only child, and life would never be the same. Bob went back to work and was occupied with making a living for his family, and it seemed like he was taking more jobs than ever just to keep out of the house. It was too difficult for him to see Scott's empty room without his school books piled on his desk or his pajamas decorating the floor. Ellen was trying to occupy herself with taking care of the home and Freddie. Many times, she would find herself polishing the silver tea set that was already sparkling from last week's cleaning. She knew Freddie was hurting, but she didn't have the energy to address it. He was no longer the noisy, happy kid, eager to talk and have a conversation. When he came home from school, he would go straight to his room. He said he was going to do his homework, but when Ellen opened his bedroom door, all she saw was her son on top of the sports comforter, fast asleep in the fetal position. His grades in school were going down, but Ellen was making all kinds of excuses for him. "He lost his brother, his best friend. Give him time. I know how he feels," she would say to Bob. "Even your sister Molly agrees with me, and you know how crazy she is about the boys. She always thought they were both perfect."

The decision to take action was made for them when Freddie's teacher requested a parent-teacher conference. "I am concerned about Freddie. His school work is poor, and he doesn't interact with the other children. He is no longer the fun-loving leader of the pack. He tries to be invisible. I realize he has experienced a terrible loss, and he probably needs some help. I believe he's thinking something but not expressing it. Perhaps you should talk to him or see a therapist."

Ellen and Bob thanked the teacher for her concern and appreciated her interest in Freddie. When Freddie came home from school that day, Ellen and Bob were waiting for him at the kitchen table.

When he arrived home, he started to retreat to his bedroom.

"Freddie, don't go upstairs yet. We want to talk to you. Sit down. I made your favorite: chocolate pudding. How was school today?"

"I have to do my homework. I have a test tomorrow. I'm not hungry," Freddie said. "Besides, chocolate pudding was Scott's favorite—not mine. Did you forget that already? Why did you do it?"

"Do what?" his parents asked while reaching out to hug him.

Freddie said, "Why did you do it? I hate both of you."

Ellen and Bob didn't know what to do or say. It was already past midnight when everyone went to bed without their dinner, and with the meatballs still in a pot on the stove, with nothing resolved and heavy hearts. Ellen was too upset to sleep. When she went into Freddie's room to check on him, Freddie was looking at the cracks in the ceiling with his flashlight.

"Are you hungry, Freddie?" she asked. "How about a sandwich?"

"Okay."

They went down to the kitchen, and Ellen made Freddie a peanut-butter-and-jelly sandwich on white bread.

Freddie ate his sandwich, and Ellen sat with him without saying a word. The house was dark, and only the sounds of the kitchen clock interrupted their thoughts.

"Why did you do it, Mom?" asked Freddie.

"Do what, Freddie?"

"Give away his heart? A kid in my class said if you give away a heart, you can't go to heaven. Besides, Scott was the best brother anyone could ever have, and now I will never see him again. I miss him."

"Your friend has the wrong information. That is not true," said Ellen. "Scott will be sitting in the most important and most beautifully carved chair in all of heaven because he gave a stranger a new life, his heart. He will be the president of heaven. Scott is a superhero. In fact, you know how he liked to help Dad with the wiring on Halloween? Well, he is probably in charge of lighting the twinkling stars at night, and he is the brightest star in the sky. Scott is the brightest star, and you can see him every night and talk to him."

"Are you sure?"

"Yes. I have never been so sure about anything in my whole life. I am 100 percent positive."

Freddie got up from his chair, put the dishes in the sink, and started to walk away with a little swagger in his step.

"Where are you going, Freddie?"

"To sleep. Good night, Mom. I have school tomorrow—plus

a test—and I can't wait to tell my friend that my brother, Scott, is the president of heaven."

"And?"

"And he is the brightest star in the sky. Why didn't you tell me this before?"

Ellen managed a rare smile. Although she made up the story to make Freddie happy, the idea that Scott was the brightest star in the sky—and that she knew where to find him and could see him—appealed to her. She knew that Scott had the potential to be president of something someday, so why not heaven? For the first time in a long time, she felt good. "Wait, Freddie," she said. "Don't go to bed yet. Let's go outside, find the brightest star, and say good night to Scott."

"Now?" he said.

"Yeah, now. Like they say, there's no time like the present."

Ellen and Freddie found a clear, starry sky when they went out on the deck. They both started to scan the sky and saw the brightest one almost immediately.

"There he is." Freddie pointed to a cluster of stars, jumped up and down, and waved. "Hi, Scott. It's me, your brother, Freddie. I can see you. I hope you can see me. I miss you. Look, Mom. He's right in the middle of all those other stars, lighting up the sky. They must be his friends. Maybe he has a girlfriend."

"Maybe," Ellen said. "I'm glad to see that he has made friends, but I know you are still his best friend."

The brightest star was twinkling on that beautiful star-studded night.

"Mom, Scott is winking at me."

"He's saying good night to you," Ellen said. "Go ahead and wink back. I think he will like that."

"Good night, Scott. I miss you every day. Mom made chocolate pudding tonight, and I told her it was your favorite.

I sleep with your Yankee teddy bear and keep it company until you come home. I hope it is okay. I will look for you tomorrow night and every night."

"Freddie, you know that Scott died, don't you?"

"Duh. Of course, Mom. I'm not an idiot." Freddie raised his eyebrows.

"Well, Freddie, when you die, your body never comes home again—just the memory and spirit of Scott remains forever. He will never come home to get his Yankee teddy bear. I am sure he would want you to have it and keep it company forever. As long as Scott remains in our memory, he will live forever."

"I know all that, Mom. I just didn't want Scott to feel bad that I had his teddy bear if he missed it."

Ellen kissed the top of his head and lovingly touched his soft cheek.

They blew kisses to Scott, went inside, and felt much more complete.

CHAPTER 11

The metal bleachers in the Printab Academy's gym were filled to capacity. It looked as if folding chairs might have to be dragged in to accommodate everyone. The spectators were carrying blankets or towels to cover the cold metal seats before they sat down. It was the night of the big basketball game. Mark's undefeated eighth-grade class against J. Benjamin Middle School, another Verona school. Both teams were all geared up for the rivalry match, proudly wearing their uniforms.

The Goldman family was in full attendance, including aunts, uncles, and cousins. David, Isabel, and Al were all about the same age and attended the same school. They volunteered to help the moms set up the aluminum folding refreshment table with Gatorade and assorted snacks that would be sold at halftime.

Isabel and Al had their eye on Dorothy's specialty: cookie brownies in a big basket. They knew they would be offered a cookie or two when their job was done. The sale of refreshments was usually a big moneymaker for the team, especially when there was a full house. In the past, the money helped pay for a new scoreboard.

The gym smelled like sweat, and the boys marched in like

a proud Olympic team. The crowd cheered and stood as they made their entrance.

Mark was tall for his age and usually played forward. He gave an uncharacteristic wave to his family when he entered with his team. The gym was decorated with large posters that wished Printab's team good luck. There was a lot of pressure on the boys to win since they were undefeated and wanted to keep their ranking in the league. The coaches, fathers of the boys on the team, gathered the players in a huddle to pep them up and to give them their instructions before the game began.

"Do your best, boys. Remember to pass to one another and don't hog the ball. You are good players, and you play well as a team. You can win this game. Go get them—and have fun."

The teammates got into their traditional huddle and put their hands together in the center.

The captain yelled, "Printab!" and the boys yelled, "Win!"

They took their places on the court and joined the spectators in the Pledge of Allegiance.

The first few minutes of the game were uneventful and scoreless.

A forward from J. Benjamin fell, hurt his knee, and was taken out of the game. He was their best player, which gave Printab an immediate advantage.

By the end of the first quarter, Printab was winning 12–2, and Mark had made a three-pointer.

The noise level in the gym was rising. David was on his feet, cheering the team and his brother for every move. He was so excited and happy to be there. The only thing that would have made him happier was if he had been playing.

In the second quarter, Printab scored several points. J. Benjamin kept making mistakes by fouling the players, giving Printab the chance to score foul shots. They excelled in this area and accumulated twelve extra points, bringing the score to

20–2 at halftime. It looked as if J. Benjamin's team was tiring and losing cohesiveness.

At halftime, the refreshment stand was doing well. David ran over to say hello to his brother and give him a high five. "I think you are going to win!"

The third quarter was even better for Printab. The team was passing the ball as they were taught and doing a great job of dribbling, making layups, and jumping to steal J. Benjamin's passes. They were on a roll.

Upon entering the last quarter, the score was 28–6 in Printab's favor, and they were continuing to have success with their rebounds. A win looked like a possibility.

One of Mark's coaches blew his whistle, and the referee stopped the game. His two coaches walked across the court to speak to J. Benjamin's coaches. All four coaches shook hands, patted each other on the back, and spoke for a few minutes, each one smiling and nodding.

The referee joined the group, nodded, and blew his whistle.

J. Benjamin picked up two more points before Mark's coach blew his whistle for their final time-out. The coach signaled for Mark to approach him.

Mark smiled, nodded, shook hands with the coach, and took off his shirt.

The announcer said, "Replacing number 18, Mark Goldman, is David Goldman."

Mark jogged over to the bleachers where David was sitting and handed him his shirt. "Come on, Bones. You are going to play basketball in my uniform." Mark smiled, took David's hand, and coaxed him off the bleachers.

David's mouth flew open, and he stared at Mark. "What? I don't understand. Is this a joke?"

"You heard the announcement. You are on the team. Come on. You are holding up the game. Get moving and get us some more points, number eighteen." Mark was beaming, and his brown eyes were twinkling.

David looked at Dorothy. She was stunned to silence, but a smile formed on her lips. She looked at Evan, not knowing if she should allow David on the court. Evan had been contacted before the game and knew what was happening. The plan was that if Printab had a big lead in the fourth quarter, the coach was going to put David in the game. The coach had heard that David had wanted to play basketball when he got his healthy heart.

"Let him play. He will be all right. No one is going to push him or touch him," Evan said.

Dorothy said, "Okay, David, but be careful. Have fun!"

With Mark's help, David put on his brother's jersey, which went down to his knees, and Mark escorted him onto the court.

David was bouncing happily all the way.

"You can do this, Bones," Mark said as he gave him an affectionate slap on his rear end.

The cheers from his family were loud and strong. The other spectators were not sure of what was happening. The team greeted him, and the game resumed without giving David any instructions. David remained on the court, but he stood to the side.

One of the Printab players threw the ball to the tall, dark-haired, athletic captain of the team. The captain had a clear shot to the basket, but instead of shooting, he threw the basketball to David.

David caught the ball

"Shoot," yelled the captain.

David looked a little bewildered. He watched for a signal from a team member, not getting one, he took a shot and the ball hit the backboard. J. Benjamin retrieved the rebound and got a two-pointer. A Printab player stole J. Benjamin's ball, and the ball was thrown directly to the captain. Again, he threw the ball to David.

"Shoot," yelled the captain when David had the ball.

David took a shot, and it bounced off the rim.

The captain caught the rebound and threw the ball to David. "Shoot!"

Everyone in the gym got the picture, and everyone shouted, "Shoot!" All the spectators were rooting for him. The ball hit the rim again, and J. Benjamin got the rebound. Instead of shooting, the player threw the ball to Printab's captain. He got a loud round of applause.

The captain threw the ball to David.

Everyone yelled, "Shoot!"

David situated himself for an overhead shot on the right side of the basket. He placed both of his hands on the ball, and with all of his strength, he jumped and aimed for the basket. The ball hit the rim and looked like it was going to fall into the basket. As it danced around the rim, there was not a sound in the gym. All eyes watched the ball. Time stood still. Everyone held their breath until the ball slowly dropped into the net, passed through it, and hit the floor. A loud sigh was heard in the room.

David had gotten a basket. He scored two points. Every person in the gym, young and old, clapped, cheered, and chanted, "David, David, David."

He was jumping up and down to the rhythm of the noise.

His new teammates surrounded him in disbelief.

Printab's coach entered the excited group, shook David's hand, presented the basketball to him, and asked the team to sign it.

David gave all the boys a fist bump and a hug as they made the customary congratulatory line after the game. When he reached his brother, Mark scooped him up and lifted him onto his shoulders. David made a victory sign and bathed in the glory as his brother took him for a lap around the room. He had won his personal Super Bowl—along with the rest of his caring team.

12

Dorothy got up on the morning of October 29, enjoying the sun peeking through the blaze of color on the trees and feeling very grateful on David's first heart birthday, but she couldn't help thinking about his donor family. The noise coming from David's room made her laugh. He was such a happy guy watching *So You Think You Can Dance*, which he taped and danced along with the dancers on a daily basis. He loved doing this and said he was going to be on the show someday.

"Well, having a TV star in the family would be fun," said Dorothy. "You never know. I never thought he would be such a good dancer."

"What?" said Evan.

"Oh, I was just talking to myself about David's possible dancing career," said Dorothy. "On a more serious note, we must find a way to remember David's donor and celebrate his life. This must be an awful day for the family. I wonder what they are doing today. What are they thinking? We have our child today, but they just have their memories."

"You're right, but what can we do? We didn't know the donor or anything about the person. We don't even know if it was a boy or a girl. David asked me the other day if the donor was a boy or girl."

"What did you say?"

"I told him I didn't know and that it didn't matter because it was a healthy heart. It's a precious gift from a stranger who you will never meet, but your lives will be tied together forever."

"That's true. I find it odd that we don't know anything about the one person who gave our son a life. We thank people for little favors—bringing flowers, food, small gifts—but the biggest gift of all, we have no one to thank. I want to say thank you today." Dorothy sat down to have a cup of fresh decaf and read the morning newspaper. As she was flipping through the paper, her eye caught an advertisement from the florist. "Mm," she said. "Birthday, flowers, balloons. Balloons? I've got it. I have an idea. Let's have a balloon launch celebration today."

"A balloon launch? What do you mean? What's a balloon launch? Is this a Dorothy invention?"

"I'm serious. This is how I picture it. We'll invite our family over and give everyone a red balloon. Then each person, even the kids, can write a note or a message to the donor on an index card or on a piece of paper. I will punch a hole in all the cards, and we will attach them to the balloon string. If anyone wants to say something to thank the donor, they can before we release all the red balloons at the same time. What do you think?"

"I think it could work."

"Of course it will work. I love it. It will be terrific. I hope I don't cry. I'm going to make some calls. I will call my parents and my brother and see if Nancy, Isabel, and Al are free. Call your mother. You know what! I think I'll invite Emily. She has her driver's license now, and she can drive over. David will be thrilled to see her. It will be an added attraction to the celebration. Since this is David's heart's first anniversary, I will get one balloon for each person. That will be eleven, one for good luck, twelve, and two special heart-shaped balloons—one for David and one for Emily. I will call Emily before I run over to Party Fair to make sure she can come."

David and his family had befriended Emily at the Miriam Irving Memorial Hospital at the time of their transplants. Emily was a senior at Eastside High School. A virus attacked her heart, but she was fortunate to have been able to obtain a heart quickly. Otherwise, she was in good health. During their stay in the hospital, Emily and David became good friends. Emily took on a big sister role in their relationship since he was much smaller and quite a bit younger. Their friendship developed and blossomed after they left the hospital. They spoke on the phone often, discussing their medicines and biopsies and gossip about the transplant nurses and which ones gave the best blood tests.

David was overjoyed to see Emily and gave her a big hug. She brought her cousin from Verona with her. Rose was a cute, athletic blonde.

"Rose wanted to come because she had a friend who was a donor, and she thought it would be a nice way to remember him," Emily said.

"Thanks for having me, Mrs. Goldman. My friend Scott was a donor. He was in my science class at school."

"I am sorry about your friend. When did he die?" asked Dorothy.

"Let me think. Maybe about a year ago. It was right after our Science fair and about the same time as the hurricane. David, I brought you a little gift. I hope you like it." Rose handed David a package wrapped in comic strip newspaper.

David unwrapped the gift, tearing the paper into shreds.

"It's a pocket-size Sudoku puzzle book. Thanks. I love it. I just started playing it, and I can't put it down." David started flipping through the pages. "It has an inscription on the inside cover: "To my nephew, Scott Paterson, from your loving Aunt Molly."

"Oh, I didn't see that. Scott was my donor friend who I just mentioned." Rose's face turned red. "I picked it up in the cardboard donation box in the school library. This is freaky and weird—really weird."

"Do you want it back?" asked David.

"No. You keep it," replied Rose.

"Okay. Let's go inside and have some chocolate pudding with whipped cream. I asked my mom to make it for us today. Yum."

They went to the kitchen for the slightly warm chocolate pudding, which was made the old-fashioned way with milk and on top of the stove.

That afternoon, while the sky was still light, every family member plus Emily and Rose launched one red balloon with a personal note tied to it. It was beautiful and emotional to see all the red balloons drifting in the cloudless sky and being taken by the wind across the horizon to heaven to greet the donor.

Dorothy got very emotional when she thanked the donor's family for their precious gift. Her emotions were contagious, which resulted in her entire family shedding tears.

Emily was pulled into the moment and expressed her gratitude to her donor's family who she also never met, and Rose spoke briefly about her friend Scott. He was in her science class, and she was sorry she hadn't gotten to know him better.

A balloon got tangled in the branches of a Japanese cherry tree in front of David's house. David's special balloon stayed in the flawless sky for the longest time. David thought it happened because it gave his donor enough time to reach out, touch the special balloon, and read his message. "Do you think my donor will like what I wrote?"

59

"What did you write David?" asked Mark.

"I said thank you for giving me a second chance."

"Wow, that's beautiful, David," said Dorothy.

"I have another question, Mom," said David.

"What is it, honey?"

"Now that it is a year since my transplant, do you think the donor family will want to get in touch with us and meet me?"

Dorothy put her arm around David and shrugged, "I don't know," she said.

Emily looked at Dorothy with the same question in her eyes, and Dorothy returned the look and said, "I don't know either."

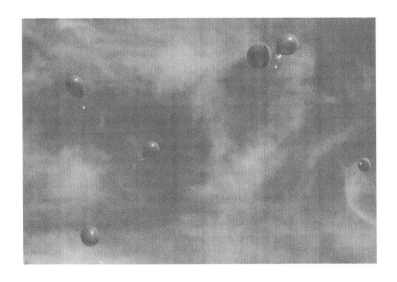

Photo taken by Max Prince

13

Molly Paterson lived in a one-bedroom condo in Verona, just a few blocks from her younger brother Bob and his family. Molly, a librarian, was not married, didn't have any children, and was very spiritual. She was interested in life after death and read all she could about it. Her two nephews, Scott and Freddie, were very important to her, and she spent a lot of time with them. Having the same color hair as they did was a sense of pride for her. She was very much part of their lives and was included in their birthdays and other family events. She knew all their friends, attended all their school functions, and was very generous in giving gifts to them. Molly was devastated when Scott died, and she mourned for him as if he was her own son. She believed in cell memory, the transfer of cells from one person to another that can happen when an organ is transplanted to another body. There are many cells in our bodies, and they retain memories about experiences, tastes, habits, and characteristics. She was sure that the recipient of Scott's heart had received some of his traits, and she needed to find the recipient. It was not an easy task.

Ellen Paterson had Freddie to distract her from her enormous sadness, but Molly did not have the distraction of another child. She marked the first anniversary of his death by posting scores of pictures of herself with Scott on Facebook. There were pictures of the two of them at Scott's birthday parties, sledding together, going out for ice cream, and break dancing in her living room.

Ellen found it very upsetting. Friends thought it was creepy and made comments to Ellen.

She knew Molly was hurting and was a good aunt to the boys, so she chose to overlook it. Physically and mentally, Ellen was in no condition for a confrontation—until she saw the most disturbing Facebook message from her sister-in-law:

> I am looking for someone who was a heart recipient during this past year who has exhibited some of the following new traits:

- new tastes in food or clothing
- a sudden interest in word puzzles, mechanics, dancing, or science

> Contact Aunt Molly

Ellen immediately called Bob. Before she could even get out one word, he said, "I know. I saw it too."

"Is she crazy? Has she lost all her marbles? What is she trying to prove?" screamed Ellen. "You better call her right now. I don't want to speak to that loony bird. She has always been a little odd. But this? Doesn't she know we are trying to heal and are not open to calls from kooky strangers like her?"

"Honey, I am in the middle of a big job. I will call her when I get home tonight."

"Okay" she said and slammed the phone down. *What is going on?* Everything around her was buzzing. The telephone was ringing, her head was whirling, and her cell phone was beeping with a text message. *Everyone in the neighborhood probably read Molly's message on Facebook and wants to clue me in. Well, I'm clued in.*

She answered the phone full of anger.

An unfamiliar male voice said, "Hi, Mom. This is Scott calling. I am in someone else's body. I will be home for dinner."

"Who is this? You little creep. Get off my phone and never call here again. If you do, I'll call the police and have you sent to prison forever." Ellen hung up and vomited all over the kitchen floor. She started to hyperventilate.

Bob had gotten the same call at work, and when he phoned Ellen—and no one answered—he rushed home. Ellen was sobbing on the kitchen floor. Her eyes were red and puffy. Bob cleaned the vomit from the floor, wiped her face, brought her a glass of water, and took her in his arms to comfort her.

After they stopped shaking and calmed down, they decided not to report the call to the police.

Ellen said, "Call your sister now and let her know all the havoc she has caused. What miserable person would make a cruel phone call like that anyway?"

"It was probably some kid in the area who saw or heard about it on Facebook and thought the phone call would be funny. A joke—some joke. The whole town knew my sister was Aunt Molly to our boys. The caller most likely got our numbers from the town directory where our home phone and my business are listed. All the residents have one—like we do. It was a prank, just a kid's prank, a prank, Ellen. This is why Facebook can be so dangerous."

Bob was boiling mad when he called his sister. "What the *hell* are you doing, Molly? Some crazy person called Ellen and said he was Scott. What do you hope to prove? Wasn't Scott's death hard enough?"

"Oh, Bob. I am so sorry. I would never do anything to hurt you and Ellen. You are the only family I have," Molly said.

"Then what is this all about?" Bob yelled.

"I miss Scott so much, and I believe some of his characteristics and traits might have been passed on to his heart recipient. I've read about cases like this. I want to have that person in my life. I need to find that person to see what part of him could be Scott. Please don't be mad at me. I did it for the love of Scott."

"Just stop it. Stop it. Don't do it again. Scott is gone," Bob screamed. "We will never forget him. We will always love him. I have a wife and Freddie to keep well now. Don't go crazy on me, Molly. I have enough on my plate." Bob banged his fist on the table.

"I won't if you say so. But what if it is true?" Molly said quietly.

"No. It is not true. It is crazy. The only thing that Scott gave to the recipient was his heart. Let it go. Ellen is so upset—and we have both been through enough."

"Okay. Bye, Scott … I mean Bob. Tell Ellen I am sorry."

Bob threw the phone across the room.

Ellen started to cry and shake again, and Bob wrapped a blanket around her shoulders.

She said, "Do you think there is any truth to what your sister said?"

"No. I don't. Let's forget this ever happened," Bob said. "Go lie down on the couch. I will bring you a cup of tea. Freddie will be home from school soon, and we want to keep him out of this."

14

The balloon launch was a great success, but Dorothy was feeling emotionally drained from the day. She and Evan went upstairs to their bedroom, which was full of family pictures.

Evan pressed the TV remote as soon as he entered the bedroom, and the space filled with the voice of Lee Goldberg from ABC News. Down the hall were the two bedrooms, one for each son.

David was relaxing and playing Sudoku on his bed and Mark was organizing his baseball cards on the carpeted floor.

Dorothy looked at Evan and said, "What's going on with David?"

"What do you mean?"

"He used to hate math and number puzzles, and now he is obsessed with Sudoku. He hardly puts it down, and he does it in ink. The next thing will be the *New York Times* crossword puzzle in ink. Yesterday, he had a chance to go to his friend's house after school, and I heard him say he couldn't go because he had to finish his Sudoku. Does that sound like our David, Mr. Social?"

"So, his likes and dislikes are changing. That's good. Don't look for trouble—trouble will look for you. There are much worse things than a Sudoku puzzle," Evan said.

"Also, chocolate pudding? I remember him gagging when I put chocolate pudding in my little glass bowls and brought them to the table. He couldn't tolerate the smell or consistency of it—and now he devours it and asks for more, and with whipped cream, which he never liked either. And he is afraid of heights and says he remembers feeling dizzy when he was on the roof. He was never on the roof. Where does that come from? Also, he is quite the little dancer, listening to music and watching himself in the mirror as he is perfecting his break dancing. He could do this all day long. He was never interested in dancing. Do you want more? Remember when he was having those terrible nightmares, and we called Dr. Deb? He was afraid to go out in that storm."

"I remember," Evan said. "Dr. Deb said it was normal for kids his age to have nightmares, and she told us we shouldn't worry."

Evan turned off the TV and said, "What are you getting at? What are you driving at? What's in that head of yours now? I'm almost afraid to ask."

"The changes started soon after his transplant—that's what I'm getting at," Dorothy said.

Evan said, "So, he started to like chocolate pudding and Sudoku after his transplant? You are being ridiculous. Just be happy that he is healthy and happy."

David walked into their room and said, "What's wrong?"

"Nothing," Evan said quickly.

"Do you like chocolate pudding?" Dorothy asked.

"I do now. I love it. I didn't before. I don't know what changed."

"Before what?" Dorothy asked.

"I don't know … maybe the transplant?"

"Enough," Evan said. "Why don't you get ready for bed and shut the door on your way out?"

"Good night, David," Dorothy said.

They both kissed his head, and he left their room.

Dorothy said, "See? Even David is able to determine the time. He might be aware of something."

Evan threw his hands up in the air. "Let's be done with this conversation. I don't want to hear anything else about this."

"Just let me tell you one more thing. Give me three minutes."

"Okay. The clock is ticking." Evan looked at his watch.

"I did some research on the internet about transplants. The article I read said that there is no scientific evidence supporting this information, but some studies attest to the theory that an organ that was transplanted can retain information from its previous owner, like transferring the donor's preference for chocolate pudding. The article even gave this phenomenon a name. The author called it cellular memory. The whole idea is just fascinating. It's on the cutting edge of a new medical discovery."

"Well, when there is some scientific evidence, talk to me again. Even if—I said if—it is true, what is there to do about it? Give back the organ and have a sick child again? In the meantime, I will say the whole idea is just plain crazy."

"Is it? Not that many years ago, we would have said a transplant is crazy—and now the procedure saved our son's life. You have misunderstood me. I don't want to do anything about it, but the theory is so interesting—and David is showing some signs. It is all so exciting," Dorothy said.

Evan held up three fingers and wiggled them. He smiled and said, "I guess we have to hope that the donor was good and smart and had a strong dislike for venison and quail if we don't want to go over our food budget. I suggest stacking up on My-T-Fine chocolate pudding and Sudoku books." Evan laughed.

Dorothy said, "Just do me a favor. Keep your eyes and ears open—and be more aware of David's activities and his likes and dislikes. Maybe they are inherited from his donor, like his dancing."

15

"Hi, Aunt Molly. This is Freddie."

"Hi my honey, I'd know your voice anywhere. I'm so happy to hear from you. I've been thinking about you. How's school? Are you playing any sports this season?"

"No, Aunt Molly, no sports this season. You know, I just couldn't. I will next year," answered Freddie.

"Yes. I know, Freddie. What's going on?"

"Aunt Molly, I want to talk to you about something."

"Sure. What is it, Freddie? Is everything all right?"

"I wanted to talk to you about the ad you put on Facebook looking for Scott's heart recipient—"

"Yes, I did it, and it caused so many problems. Some crank called your parents and said it was Scott. They were devastated. I am sorry I did it and have apologized many times. I was wrong, but I still believe in the cell memory theory and … I was wrong,"

Aunt Molly could hear Freddie's uneven heavy breathing. "Freddie, are you there?"

"Yes, I'm here," he murmured.

"What's wrong?" she asked. "I'm sorry I hurt your parents, Freddie. Are you angry at me too? Please forgive me."

Freddie mumbled a reply.

"What did you say? I can't understand you."

Freddie was crying. It started as a whimper and then developed into hysterics.

"Calm down, Freddie. I don't know what you are saying. Take a deep breath. Do you want me to come over? I am preparing dinner, but that can wait."

"I did it. I did it," he said. "I did it. I am the crank." Freddie could feel his heart heaving in his chest and his stomach doing somersaults.

"You are the crank, Freddie? You are the one who called your parents and said you were Scott? Why, Freddie? Why? Your parents love you and have been so good to you."

"I don't know," he answered. "I don't know, but it feels good to tell someone."

"You will have to tell your parents, Freddie," said Aunt Molly.

"I know, Aunt Molly. I know. I want them to punish me. I'm so ashamed. They are going to hate me and think I'm a terrible child—and maybe give me away. I'm so sorry. I love Scott. I miss my brother and want him back. Come back, Scott. Come back." The flood of tears started all over again. "Do you think they will give me away?"

"They might be mad at you, but they would never give you away. Are your parents home now?"

"Yes. They are watching TV downstairs. We just finished eating dinner."

"Okay," said Aunt Molly. "I will be over as soon as I can, and we will talk to your parents."

"Now? Today? Now?"

"Yes, now."

That evening, Ellen, Bob, Aunt Molly, and Freddie gathered in the living room. Ellen, Bob, and Freddie sat together on the comfortable couch, and Aunt Molly sat on the matching blue striped chair. Ellen and Bob, although happy to have everyone together, had no idea the reason for this powwow.

Freddie pressed his hands together and told his parents what he did. "I'm sorry. I'm sorry. Do you hate me?" Freddie reached out to hug them.

They looked at him in disbelief and wonder. Had they heard him correctly? Was he the caller who Ellen wanted locked up? They were hurt, feeling like they had been lashed with a whip.

The few minutes before anyone spoke seemed like an eternity to Freddie.

Ellen was shouting when she first spoke to Freddie, "You? You were the one? It was you on the telephone saying it was Scott. It was you? We can't believe it. Why would you do that? Why? I don't understand, I don't understand. We have been through so much. Why, why did you do it?"

"I'm sorry, Mom. I'm sorry, Dad," Freddie said. "Punish me. I love you. Punish me. Take away my iPad. I don't know why I did it. I love you."

Aunt Molly went over to Freddie and gave him a hug.

Freddie buried his face in Aunt Molly's shoulder, "I thought I could bring him back if I said I was Scott. I didn't get a chance to hug him, "he cried as she rubbed his back trying to calm him down.

Ellen and Bob knew how much he was still grieving and how confused he was about Scott's death. Still shaking from the news, they took deep breathes to calm themselves down, and went to return his hug and thank Aunt Molly for being there when he needed someone.

"We love you too, Freddie. We realize how much we all

miss Scott. I think the best thing for the family is to talk to a professional. I would like to make an appointment for all of us to see your therapist. We all could use some help. Would you like that? We were so wrapped up in our own grief that we neglected you. I am sorry."

"Yes," Freddie said. He began to smile when Ellen put her arms around him and kissed his cheek.

16

D r. Sam Maxwell had been seeing the Paterson family since Scott's death. His office was on the second floor in a building without an elevator on Bloomfield Avenue in Verona. After climbing the narrow steps, they entered a large colorful waiting room. The walls were lined with many aquariums of different sizes.

The receptionist was feeding the goldfish when they arrived. "Hi, Freddie. Hi, Mr. and Mrs. Paterson. Hey, Freddie, would you like to help me feed the fish?"

"Sure, Debbie. We have fish at home. I know what to do."

Debbie gave Freddie the container of fish food and asked Ellen and Bob to sign some papers.

"Hello, folks. It's nice to see you," Dr. Maxwell said from the doorway. Ellen and Bob, why don't you wait here while I talk to Freddie alone—and then you can join us. Debbie will get you coffee or tea. Is that okay with you, Freddie? I am going to try to beat him in checkers today."

"Sure." Freddie walked with Dr. Maxwell to his office and gave a thumbs-up sign to Ellen.

Dr. Maxwell said, "It looks like you beat me again. I am going to call you the Checker Wiz." He gave Freddie some drawing paper and crayons.

Freddie took the paper and began to draw.

"I see that you drew a big tree and a little boy. Is that a special tree?" asked Dr. Maxwell.

"That's the bad tree that killed my brother, but it didn't hurt me," answered Freddie.

"What about the boy? Is that a special boy?"

"That's me." Freddie picked up a crayon and added a cape to the boy's back.

"What did you put on your back?"

"I put a cape on my back."

"A cape?" Dr. Maxwell said. "Why?"

"Superman wears a cape, and he has special powers—and now we both have special powers."

"What special powers do you have, Freddie?"

Freddie stood up, extended his arms like Superman, and said, "Superman is going to help me bring Scott back to my family."

"Superman and you have special powers that will let you remember your brother forever. You will always remember that tree that killed Scott and not you, but we can never bring Scott's body back. As long as you remember him, he's alive for you. What did you and your brother do together?"

"Scott always helped me build things. We played ball together, and we had pillow fights when Mom wasn't looking—and a lot of other things."

"All those things are called memories. You will always have them, and nobody can ever take them away from you. You can look at pictures of Scott every day if you want, and that might help you see him."

"I have a lot of pictures of him," Freddie answered. "Maybe I can make a photo album with all the pictures."

"That sounds like a good idea. Is it okay with you if I talk to your parents for a few minutes while you can try to beat Debbie in checkers? I understand she is pretty good at the game."

Freddie went to the waiting room, and Ellen and Bob came into his office.

"Have a seat." Dr. Maxwell pointed to two comfortable chairs next to his desk. His desk was clear except for the pictures of his smiling young children. "My conversation with Freddie was a good one. I think Freddie was being honest with you and himself when he said he didn't know why he made the phone call. As you must know, there are many possibilities. We must remember that Freddie is still a child. He is still mourning his brother. He is trying to figure out this difficult concept called death—as we all are. Being the surviving child, he is now an only child and probably has a lot of anger and guilt in the position he now finds himself. There is nothing wrong with him; he is trying to work out his remorse in his own way. I am sure I can help him. He needs time and patience and the love that you give him. Do you have any questions before I ask him to come in?"

"What should we be doing to help him?"

"Be honest with him. Freddie is smart, and if you don't know the answers, tell him so. And as I said before, show him patience and love. Let's ask him to come back in now." Dr. Maxwell went out to the waiting room to get Freddie.

17

Every year, the Miriam Irving Memorial Children's Hospital has a dance for its kids—whether they are in-house or out-house patients. They call it a prom, and the administration has an all-out, sky-is-the-limit attitude toward it. The prom is held right at the hospital, although you would never guess that the beautifully decorated candlelit ballroom with a perfumed scent would be the cafeteria in the morning—and the white-gloved waitresses would be Monday's lunch aides. The reasons for hospitalization run the gamut. Some have been transplant patients, some are waiting for transplants, and others are cancer patients or have undergone surgeries. Children who are waiting to be diagnosed are not permitted to attend in case they have anything contagious.

David loves to dance, is a good dancer and is very excited about the prom. He also loves music and has great rhythm. Friends and family wondered how a child who was pretty much sedentary and isolated for his whole life could get up on the dance floor and command it. He always has an audience when he dances, clapping along and encouraging him to do his hip-hop moves. When watching him, Dorothy thought more and more that the effects from his transplant could be the answer.

David said, "Mom, do you think Emily would like to go to the prom with me and be my date?"

"The only way you will find out is to ask. Here's her number. Give her a call—maybe she likes younger men," Dorothy said with a giggle.

"No. I think I'll text her. She usually answers her texts ASAP."

Emily answered immediately, saying she would love to go.

Dorothy and Evan offered to drive them because they were nosy and wanted to be peeping toms.

The night of the prom, David got all dressed up in a tie, dark jacket, and pants. He felt like his daddy who dressed that way every day for his job at the bank. He looked so handsome with his thick brown hair slicked back. Mark got out his camera and took lots of pictures. David loved to be photographed, loved the spotlight and Mark was more comfortable behind the camera.

Dorothy and David bought a pink rose wrist corsage for Emily and a white boutonniere for David.

"What's in that bulging jacket pocket of yours, David?"

"Oh, just some peanut butter cups—my favorites—for me and Emily." David touched his pocket to make sure they were still there.

"That's nice. I thought M&Ms were your favorite."

"Not anymore, Mom, and when you go to the store, stop buying Rocky Road ice cream. I discovered Turkey Hill's Chocolate Swirl."

Dorothy looked at him intently, focusing on his words and hoping for more information.

"Since when? I have a freezer full of Rocky Road. Who is going to eat it?"

"I don't know. Give it to Mark. He'll eat it," David said.

Dorothy made a mental note of the conversation. Evan

would probably dismiss it, but it was more ammunition for the cell memory argument. *Too bad he didn't witness it.*

Emily was wearing a black sleeveless short dress with fashionable multicolored spiked heels that made their difference in height even more prominent. She looked "hot."

David gave Emily the wrist corsage, and Emily squatted down to pin the boutonniere on David's jacket. They had a lot in common and were very comfortable with one another despite the differences in age and height.

There was a long red carpet at the hospital, and the voice of Justin Timberlake was bouncing off the walls.

"Walking on the red carpet now are Mr. David Goldman and Miss Emily Samuels," boomed the voice on the loud speaker interrupting Justin Timberlake.

The crowd cheered.

Dorothy and Evan found a good spot to watch the festivities.

A young man standing next to them said, "Who is that little kid walking with that tall beautiful girl?"

They immediately answered, "That's my son."

"Wow he sure can do those hip hop moves. It must have cost you plenty to give him all those dance lessons." They both looked at David and smiled.

The food was served elegantly—like in a fine restaurant—and the menu offered chicken, turkey, pasta, and Shirley Temple cocktails with stemmed cherries hanging from the glass.

These kids certainly deserve a party like this with all they have gone through thought Dorothy.

During dessert, David's watch beeped. He looked at the time and saw he needed to take his antirejection medicine.

Emily's medication was on the same schedule as David's. She opened her little black purse and took her medicine.

Within seconds of taking the medicine, David and Emily got phone messages from their moms to remind them to take their meds.

"I don't think they trust us, "said Emily.

Emily and David danced all evening and enjoyed every minute. They took breaks to rest and when the beautiful meal was served.

David danced in the middle of a circle of admiring spectators who were cheering him on. His body moved so gracefully and smoothly when he was on the dance floor. When he was dancing, he was in his element.

Dorothy and Evan went to a diner for Greek salads and cheesecake. They wanted to head home fairly early because the kids had another big event the next day. It was the annual 5K walk and race for the New Jersey Sharing Network for Tissue and Organ Donations.

"Why does all the good stuff happen at the same time?" asked David.

"That's the way the cookie crumbles," Dorothy said. "Did you have a good time?"

"It was awesome."

"Okay. Then, you can look forward to it again next year. Let's go. We have to be out very early tomorrow morning to set up our tent at the Sharing Network. You will see Emily again tomorrow."

18

T he 5K walk and race attracted approximately six thousand people from New York and New Jersey. They came from all walks of life. David's family planned on setting up a tent for all their guests to gather and eat bagels, muffins, and granola bars before the race.

Mark was tall and strong, and he helped Evan lug all the paraphernalia from the parking lot. They carried the aluminum refreshment table plus the food , drinks and the blue soccer chairs for their teammates. They were worn out even before the race began.

Mark volunteered to be a team captain for David's team of friends and family. For his upcoming Bar Mitzvah, Mark was required to get involved in a mitzvah project—to do something good for other people. His job as a team captain was a good choice because the New Jersey Sharing Network affected him and his family personally. He took this project very seriously by helping organize the event with his mother and fund-raising. Everyone was very generous, and their team was one of the top ten fund-raisers. They had seventy friends of all ages join David's team.

Parents pushing strollers, senior citizens, and school friends were all wearing red short-sleeved shirts to support

David. Most of the participants in the noisy crowd were donor families, and they were walking in memory of loved ones who had died and donated organs. It was heart-wrenching and at the same time beautiful to see masses of people walking together and carrying large banners and photographs of loved ones whose memories were being honored. Their names were announced over the loudspeaker as they crossed the yellow finish line. The recipient families walked tall and strong, reflecting their gratitude.

David's physical therapist pulled him in his rusted Red Flyer wagon, which was rescued from the garage so he could participate in his first 5K. All seventy members walked the course together, talking, drinking from their water bottles, and having a good time.

When they neared the end, David jumped out of the wagon and crossed the finish line—smiling from ear to ear— on the shoulders of Uncle Dan.

The crowd roared. It was a spectacular moment to witness. Seeing these healthy children and adults walking the course revealed exactly what donating organs was all about—and the difference it made in life. It made such an impact on the attendees that David's picture was captured on camera by many photographers. His picture appeared on the front page of the newspaper the following day along with a story about the Sharing Network. David was a celebrity, and he loved every bit of it.

19

On the first anniversary of Scott Paterson's death, Ellen Paterson didn't have to look at the calendar to know the date. She could feel it in the air and in her bones. She could tell her husband was trying to do something nice by the way the smell of fresh coffee greeted her when she went into the kitchen for breakfast. The table was set, the coffeepot was already gurgling, and her favorite cheese Danish was in the breadbasket in the center of her placemat.

"Good morning. Where did the yummy-looking Danish come from?" Ellen said pretending to be jovial.

"From the bakery. I went out early this morning with Molly to get them. I got them hot out of the oven. Boy, did they smell good. You wouldn't believe how many people frequent the bakery so early in the morning. I thought you could use something special to start your day." Bob gave Ellen a peck on her cheek. "It was really Molly's idea. I think she is trying to make amends. She wanted to join us for breakfast, but I told her I didn't think it was a good idea. Especially today. I told her maybe next weekend."

"You were right to say no for today. She has apologized many times, and I know she didn't do it to be mean. I will try to give her a call next week."

Ellen and Bob had a tough time getting through the first year after Scott's death. They were determined to make it and keep their family whole. Every week, they went to see a couple's therapist who specialized in loss and grief. They both felt guilty, and the important thing they learned—and were still working on—was not blaming one another. The big oak tree that fell was scheduled to be taken down. It was providing too much shade, and they wanted more sun in the front of their house. But it rained on the tree guy's scheduled day, and neither of them returned his calls to schedule another appointment. After Scott's death, they were blaming themselves and each other plus fighting by hurling insults at one another. It was getting mean and ugly.

The therapist encouraged them to talk to one another about the accident and to keep all communication alive and open. The insults and the blame weren't helping anyone. Their marriage had a strong foundation, and they loved each other. Every so often, Freddie would join them in the therapy session. He was working through the loss of his older brother. Ellen and Bob knew that there was a high divorce rate among couples who lost a child, and they didn't want to fall into that category.

"Thanks honey," Ellen said. "That was very thoughtful of you. It tastes delicious. Have one, Bob. I can't eat all of them—well, maybe I can. All kidding aside, dig in."

"What would you like to do today? I am all yours. I cleared my calendar and am free the whole day," Bob said while nibbling his cheese Danish and sipping his coffee.

"I don't know," said Ellen. "I don't feel like doing anything. Maybe we should just hang low, give Freddie a treat, and go out for a bite to eat tonight. Remember that our therapist told us not to forget Freddie. He is important, and he is also our son. He also suffered a loss. Don't be upset. I want to tell you something that has been going around in my head. I've been thinking for some time now that I would like to know more about Scott's organ recipient. I hope the child is well and happy, I assume it is a child, and I wonder if he or she is mechanical like Scott or anything like Scott. Remember how we loved to watch Scott dance as soon as he heard music? Wouldn't that be funny and miraculous at the same time? Where does the recipient live? How old is the person? What does the child look like? Maybe it's a boy with red hair and a freckled face. I have so many unanswered questions. I think it would be helpful to me to find out some of these answers."

"Whoa, Ellen. Slow down. You never mentioned any of this before—not even in our therapy sessions." Bob raised his eyebrows. "I knew it was bound to come up sooner or later."

"I know. I have been thinking, but I never said it out loud before." Ellen looked at Bob and said, "Would you like to find out more about the person?"

Bob thought for a long time. "Yes, certainly. I always think about it. It's always in my thoughts, but I don't know if I am ready yet. We are still working on our other issues—just learning to live without Scott and making sure Freddie is well. Meeting someone with Scott's heart would be wonderful. It would be a continuation of him. We decided to donate his heart to give someone a new life and help keep Scott's memory alive for us. It was the right decision, and I would make the same decision again. I just need a little more time. Also, let's talk to Freddie about this to see if he is ready."

That afternoon, Bob and Freddie were watching television on the brown couch in the TV room.

Ellen said, "I'm making you guys a treat. How about popcorn?"

"It smells terrific," said Freddie when he got a whiff of the aroma coming from the kitchen.

Ellen emptied the popcorn into a big plastic bowl and brought it to the boys.

"Eat it slowly because I am only making one bag. We are going to go out for pizza tonight." She put the bowl on the table and sat next to Freddie on the couch.

"That sounds cool. Hey, Dad, when are we going to put up our Halloween decorations? It is almost Halloween. I can give you a hand carrying up the boxes from the basement." Freddie flexed his bicep. "The Halloween stuff is in big brown cartons, the kind for fruits and vegetables in the supermarket. I know exactly where to find them, under the steps. I think there are only two or three boxes. It'll be a cinch."

Bob said, "I don't know, Freddie. I really wasn't planning on decorating this year. The loss of Scott is still too raw, and we always decorated and strung the wiring together. I'm sorry, Freddie."

"I know how you feel, but I would like do it with you, Dad. I've watched you and Scott for years. I can do it. Maybe we can hang only one strip of lights, and we can even change the colors. It will look different. Scott will be disappointed when he doesn't see any lights on our lawn. He will think that we forgot about him." Freddie moved closer to his dad and put his hand on his shoulder.

Ellen cleared her throat and winked at Bob.

"Okay," Bob said. "You've got a deal. We'll go out and buy all different color lights and string them together. I will teach you how to make them flash." Bob extended his hand for a handshake.

"That's a deal, Dad." Freddie smiled as they shook hands and then hugged.

Ellen smiled and said, "If you go now, you can be back before it's time to go to the restaurant,"

Freddie said, "I can taste that pizza already. I think I'll have mine with pepperoni."

20

Bob and Freddie climbed into the Bob's work truck and headed to Home Depot.

Freddie opened the window and said, "Scott loved this time of year."

"You're right, Freddie. He certainly did. I remember him telling me that he loved the smell of autumn. Now when I go outside on a clear fall day, I think of Scott. I imagine you and Scott playing in the leaves just like you did when you were little. It makes me happy. It is a good memory to hold onto." Bob pulled into the crowded parking lot, turned off the engine, and said, "Before we go in, I would like your opinion on something."

"You want my opinion?" answered Freddie. For a minute, he imagined himself smoking an expensive cigar with his feet on a large desk and a secretary recording his every word in a spectacular office that said "Freddie Paterson, President" on the door. "Sure, how can I help you, Dad?" He stopped fumbling with his iPhone and gave Bob his full attention.

"I'll give it to you straight, man to man—or better yet, father to son. What do you think? Would you like to meet the recipient of Scott's heart?"

After several minutes, Freddie said, "Today?"

"No, Freddie. Not today. It could be next week, next month, or even next year at some point."

"I've always thought about what it would be like to meet the person for the first time. I've thought about what I would say and do. Should I give the person a hug or a handshake or even a high five like I did with Scott? If it is a girl, should I give her a kiss? What should I do, Dad? Will that person be my brother if he has Scott's heart?" Freddie began playing with his iPhone again. "Will the person look like me and Scott with red hair and freckles?" He checked his reflection in the mirror.

"The person who has Scott's heart is not necessarily a boy. You are right. It could be a girl," Bob said.

"Then I could have a new brother or sister? Is that right?" Freddie began to snicker.

"What's so funny, son?" Bob asked.

"I'm picturing a girl with red hair and freckles who looks like Scott," Freddie said with a laugh. "A tall, skinny girl who likes to build robots and string Halloween lights when she is not dancing—and does Sudoku in the dark. Wouldn't that be a riot?"

"That would be funny. Even Mom would get a chuckle out of that one." Bob said with a big grin. "Whoever it turns out to be, I want you to remember now and always that your brother Scott loved you very much."

"I know that, Dad, but it is nice to hear," answered Freddie.

"You are asking very grown-up philosophical questions for a kid your age. All I can tell you is that, if you want to, you can love the person like a brother or sister, but by birth, you only have one brother—and that is Scott. The rest is up to you," Bob said with tears forming in his eyes.

"What do you and Mom think? I want to hear your opinions now."

"Well, we both think it is a good idea, and we both are

eager to meet the recipient who deserves the opportunity of getting to know us—his donor's family. However, we have a difference of opinions. I am not quite ready yet, and Mom is ready now."

"I think I feel like Mom. I am ready now. I am curious about who the person is and what he or she looks like. Maybe we will be friends—not brothers, but friends. Let's go in and get the lights now. I don't want to miss our dinner."

CHAPTER 21

Dorothy opened the refrigerator and looked for something to make for dinner. She had been so preoccupied with the launch that she hadn't gone food shopping in a couple of days. She looked at the empty shelves and said, "Let's go to Franco's for dinner. First of all, I don't feel like cooking—plus there's nothing to eat unless you want ketchup and mayo on white bread. Secondly, we can celebrate David's heart birthday. What do you say?"

"I'm in," said Mark.

David said, "Me too—and let's wear our Donate Life shirts that we got at the race. We'll look important."

"No, we won't," Mark said. "We will look stupid—all walking in wearing the same shirt. I'm not wearing mine."

"Mark, we won't look stupid. Go and put it on. You should be proud to wear the shirt. We all finished the race, didn't we? That's an accomplishment, even though my body still aches. Also, it's a worthwhile organization. It's committed to saving lives, like your brother's, through educating people about organ donations and giving support to donor families after their loss. I am going to do volunteer work for them."

"Okay, Mom. Okay. Okay. I hear you, but you owe me big-time!" Mark said in a huff.

"How does a Nutella pizza sound?" Dorothy rubbed her tummy in jest.

Mark said, "It sounds good, but that's not exactly what I call big-time, and I don't know if Franco's makes a Nutella pizza."

"We'll see," Dorothy said.

"Go change. Let's go now. I'm hungry." Evan grabbed his shirt and headed out to the car.

Franco's was crowded, and they had to wait before they were seated at a table in the back. They were wearing their white Donate Life shirts with blue and green lettering.

"It looks like they are giving away food. What's happening tonight?" Dorothy asked. She opened the menu and saw they had a Halloween pizza special. "Now I know it's cheaper to eat out with the special than to cook."

"Is Nutella pizza on the menu?" asked Mark.

"I don't see it, but I will ask the waitress."

"What are you looking at, Dorothy?" asked Evan. "The waitress is coming over now to take our order."

"I am looking over there." She pointed to a man at another table.

"Where is over there?"

"That man over there looks familiar," she whispered. "The man wearing the blue baseball cap at the round table near the door with the woman and boy. He's talking to the waitress now."

"The boy is Freddie. His brother was in my Boy Scout troop," Mark whispered.

"What do you mean *was*?" Dorothy asked.

"He's the one who died before Halloween when we had the big storm. Don't you remember? I told you our troop collected money and sent a dozen yellow roses from Flower World."

"Oh no. I remember now. They were in the lounge in the

hospital the day David got his new heart. Their son had just died. I thought he looked familiar. I think his wife was still in shock when I saw her. Evan, that's when you went to get coffee."

Dorothy's eyes glazed over. "I remember the conversation: 'My son died today. I had two sons. I had two sons. What brings you here? The heart is here.' Oh my God. I can picture it now."

"What's the matter, honey," Bob said.

"Never mind. I was just remembering something strange, something impossible, very impossible. Forget it."

David said, "It looks like Freddie sees you, Mark. He is giving you a wave. Wave back."

Mark waved back.

Freddie leaned over and said, "Mom, I am going to say hello to someone who was in Scott's Boy Scout troop."

"Who?" Ellen asked.

"Mark Goldman, he's in the back with his family."

"Which ones?"

"The ones wearing the Donate Life shirts," Freddie answered.

"I have a Donate Life shirt at home. It came in the mail when we donated Scott's organs. I never took it out of the package. It's still in the closet."

"I didn't know that," Bob said.

Seeing the Donate Life shirts brought a rush of memories to Ellen of the evening in the hospital and the question of whether to donate Scott's organs. They arrived at the hospital a year ago as broken people, parents who had experienced the worst thing possible, losing child. Then the question of donating organs was posed to them.

First, they got very angry. How could such a question be

asked when they had just lost part of their lives, their beautiful young son? No one should experience such a tragedy. They didn't want to think about it. They didn't want to talk about it, and they told the doctor to leave the room immediately.

Although filled with anguish and heartache, Bob and Ellen knew deep down that someone would benefit from their son's healthy, young organs. It was a topic that was never discussed, but they knew that Scott—with his scientific mind, love of science, and the goodness in his heart—would approve of it. Everything was such a shock that evening, and the decision had to be made quickly.

Scott's death was such a senseless one; at least it was something good for them to always remember. They believed Scott would be alive in someone else's body and his organs would prevent another family from going through this loss, which they found comforting.

When the medical staff and a representative from the New Jersey Sharing Network asked for their decision about donating his organs, they gave an affirmative answer and signed the papers. The image of signing those papers, which characterized the finality of Scott's life and the feeling of the pit in her stomach and her broken heart, would always remain in Ellen's mind.

Ellen looked at her husband and said, "It's still difficult."

"I know that, honey. It is for me too." Bob touched Ellen's hand.

Ellen said, "I feel strange even coming to a restaurant today of all days. I know we said we would do it for Freddie to begin to bring some normalcy in our lives and celebrate Scott's life, but it doesn't feel right." She turned to Freddie and said, "Do you have to go over to see him now? I'm not going over. I'm in no mood to talk to strangers."

"Oh, let him go, Ellen. Just say hello, Freddie, and come right back," Bob said.

Freddie went to say hello.

Bob said, "That lady with the Donate Life shirt looks awfully familiar."

"Everyone always looks familiar to you," Ellen said.

"No. I've seen her before. There's something about her, but I can't figure it out."

Freddie returned to the table and said, "Was that quick enough?"

"Good boy, Freddie." Bob patted his son on the back.

"Mark's mother asked me to join them, but I told her I couldn't. They are all wearing the same shirts. I let them know that my mother has a Donate Life shirt too. She acted kind of funny when I said it. She asked me when you got it, and I told her a year ago when my brother died."

"Now I remember." Bob shook his head.

"Remember what?" Ellen asked.

They were in the cardiac lounge. When we were leaving the hospital the man said," What brings you here?"

I answered ,"My son is in surgery."

The family at the table was smiling and laughing with tears in their eyes as the waitress brought out a heart-shaped cake. They all sang "Happy Birthday."

Bob looked at Ellen, and Ellen looked at Bob. "Could it be?"

Ellen lost all the color in her face.

Bob shouted, "Get Mom a drink of water—and make it quick."

Smiling David Goldman put a piece of his red-frosted heart-shaped birthday cake on their table with a folded napkin. A small Sudoku book fell out of his pocket.

Ellen looked at the piece of cake and the napkin as if she expected them to explode.

Bob picked up the book and saw Scott's name in his handwriting on the cover. He clasped it tightly to his chest and said to Ellen, "Open the napkin. There is something written on it. What does it say?"

Ellen's fingers trembled as she opened the napkin and looked up to see David's beautiful smiling face and his freckled nose.

In large print, there were two words: "THANK YOU."

EPILOGUE

It is time to reopen life's three-ringed blank notebook and chronicle the events for Scott Paterson and David Goldman, the two strangers who never met but whose lives and families are intertwined until eternity.

Scott's book closed the day he died when the tree fell and killed him. However, the heartache his parents and brother are experiencing because of his loss will follow them to the last chapters of their books. Even though Ellen's and Bob's books are filled with sadness, they are mixed with many happy times that they experienced together and with Freddie and their new family. Through the unselfish heart donation of Scott and his family to a complete stranger, his memory and goodness will live on forever through David Goldman. The Patersons' books will become part of the Goldmans' story for many generations, and Scott will not be forgotten.

David Goldman's book has many pages and chapters added to his original birth book. Modern science and a heart transplant have allowed him do things that seemed impossible on the day he was born: play basketball, dance, travel, and live a normal life with his grateful family.

This happened through the generosity of Scott—a stranger whose heart and possibly traits live within David's body.

Aunt Molly smiled and was thrilled when she heard that Scott's heart recipient was found. Now she could test her cell memory theory and be reunited with her nephew.

Life continues, and we are all part of one another's stories.

GLOSSARY

AORTA. The blood vessel that carries the blood away from the heart to the rest of the body; the largest artery in the body.

BIOPSY. The removal of a sample of tissue for examination under the microscope for abnormalities.

CARDIAC. Having to do with the heart.

CARDIOLOGIST. A doctor who treats the heart. A pediatric cardiologist is a doctor who treats children's hearts.

CELLULAR MEMORY. An organ recipient acquires traits from the donor though the transfer of the memory in cells.

CHRONIC. A condition that lasts a long time.

CIRCULATION. A movement of blood through the heart and around the body. It takes less than sixty seconds to pump blood to every cell in your body.

COMPLICATION. An unanticipated problem.

CONGENITAL. A condition present at birth whether it is inherited or not.

CYANOSIS. A bluish color of the skin due to insufficient oxygen.

DONOR. A giver of a tissue or organ.

ECHOCARDIOGRAM. A diagnostic test that uses ultrasound waves to make images of the parts of the heart. It does not hurt.

ELECTROCARDIOGRAM (EKG). Records the heart's electrical activity. Sticky pads (electrodes) are placed on the chest and hooked up to a machine that records the heart activity on a paper. The doctor determines if the heart is normal. It does not hurt.

HEART. The muscle that pumps blood from the veins into arteries and throughout the body. It is the size of a fist.

HEART TRANSPLANT. A surgical procedure that removes a diseased heart and replaces it with a healthy heart.

HYPOPLASTIC LEFT HEART SYNDROME (HLHS). A serious and rare congenital disease that does not allow normal blood flow through the heart.

IMMUNE SYSTEM. A complex system that is responsible for protecting the body against foreign substances.

ORGAN. An independent part of the body that carries out one or more specific functions, like lungs, heart, and liver.

OXYGEN. An odorless gas that is present in the air for life. In a medical setting, it can be delivered through nasal tubes.

REJECTION. When the body's immune system attacks transplanted cells or organs.

SURGERY. The branch of medicine that does operations to cure a disease or infection.

VEINS. Looks blue and returns blood to the heart, while arteries look red and carry blood away from the heart.

Printed in the United States
By Bookmasters